L. C Searle

Washington - Our Example

The Father of a Nation will Restore it to Peace

L. C Searle

Washington - Our Example
The Father of a Nation will Restore it to Peace

ISBN/EAN: 9783337220730

Printed in Europe, USA, Canada, Australia, Japan

Cover: Foto ©Andreas Hilbeck / pixelio.de

More available books at **www.hansebooks.com**

WASHINGTON, OUR EXAMPLE.

THE FATHER OF A NATION

WILL

RESTORE IT TO PEACE.

BY MRS. L. C. SEARLE.

'Providence appointed Washington childless that America might call him father."

Upon War.—"My first wish is to see this plague of mankind banished from the earth, and the sons and daughters of this world employed in more pleasing and innocent amusements, than in preparing instruments, and exercising them for the destruction of mankind."—*George Washington.*

PHILADELPHIA:

JAMES CHALLEN & SON,

1865.

"Has the Birthday of Washington any lesson to us? The nation of which he was the leader, in its struggle for birth and place among the nations of the earth, has been for three years carrying on a struggle for existence, compared with which the toils and pains of that early conflict are not to be named. Have we lost in the heat of the conflict any thing of the veneration with which we think of the hero whose birth we celebrate to-day? Are we losing sight of things which he held dear, and setting at naught the principles for which his days of toil and nights of anxiety were spent? There are those among us who claim that we are, and say that the dominant party has no desire to keep Washington before the country as a father, a teacher, or an example."—*N. Y. Times*, Feb. 22d, 1864.

"As the Copperheads profess to hold the memory of Washington in the highest respect, and to regard him as a model patriot and an immaculate statesman, we hope to be pardoned for suggesting to them that a slight study of the life and character of their idol might add biographical accuracy to their lucubrations. Washington was human, and had his share of human infirmities. We claim Washington as an abolitionist. The Virginia slaveholders were nearer the infancy of the republic than we are. They knew what doctrine of human equality the Revolution was intended to vindicate and establish; they felt as we can never feel the pressure of strictly logical conclusions."—*N. Y. Tribune*, Feb. 22d, 1864.

"When God resolved to set his people free from Egyptian bondage, he raised up able and mighty men to effect his glorious purposes. There is a striking resemblance between the history of the Israelites and that of the American colonies. Like Moses, Washington led his countrymen through the dreary wilderness of the Revolution, and planted them on the promised land of freedom. Like Moses, he placed his trust in the God of Hosts, and relied upon his special aid and direction under all circumstances."—*Mrs. Willard.*

3

WHEN Washington drew his sword in defence of America against the tyranny of George the Third and the British Parliament, white men of all nations were welcomed to the standard unfurled for liberty and independence. France sent her Marquis de Lafayette, Prussia her Baron Steuben, Poland her noble Kosciusko, who, with many more of their own countrymen, as well as those of other nations, crossed the ocean and offered their services to the warrior, fighting for the freedom of his country. The Americans hailed these friends of liberty from foreign lands with gratitude and joy, and numbers were appointed to positions of honor and trust.

But already in America, dwelling close at hand in every colony, was a race of men, numbered by hundreds of thousands, who received no greeting of welcome into the army, but were positively forbidden to enlist under the banner of the "Father of his Country." In his "Orderly Book," bearing the date of 1775, there still stands recorded this prohibition: "No negroes, or boys unable to bear arms, or old men, are to be enlisted." The black race from Africa, which had been forced among our ancestors by the English government while engaged in the African Slave Trade, was not only thus excluded by Washington, the Commander-in-Chief, from a place by the side of the white race, as soldiers in his army, but by the laws of the American people;

5

and in two instances only was there any deviation from this established order during eight long years of war with their powerful and haughty foe.

In June, 1775, General Washington was sent to the relief of Massachusetts, the harbor of Boston having been blockaded by a British fleet, and in December following he wrote to Congress as follows: "It has been represented to me that the free negroes, who have served in the army at Cambridge, are very much dissatisfied at being discarded. As it is to be apprehended that they may seek employ in the ministerial army, I have presumed to depart from the resolution respecting them, and have given license for their being enlisted. If this is disapproved of by Congress, I will put a stop to it." Mr. Sparks, the publisher of the writings of Washington, explains the above letter as follows: "At a meeting of the general officers previously to the arrival of the Committee from Congress in camp, it was unanimously resolved that it was not expedient to enlist slaves into the new army, and by a large majority, negroes of every description were excluded from enlistment. When the subject was referred to the Committee in conference, this decision was confirmed. In regard to free negroes, however, the resolve was not adhered to, and probably for the reason here mentioned by Washington."

Bancroft throws additional light on the subject. He says:

"In October, 1775, the conference in the camp of the army at Boston, with Lynch, Harrison and Franklin, thought it proper to exclude negroes from the new enlistment, but Washington, at the crisis of his distress, finding that those who had entered the army at the beginning were very much dissatisfied at being discarded, took the responsibility of reversing this decision and referred the subject to Congress. That body appointed Wythe, Wilson and Samuel Adams, to deliberate on the question. On the report of this able Committee, Congress voted that the free negroes who had served faithfully in the army, at Cambridge, might be enlisted therein, but no others."

Here are the facts of history, that in "his crisis of distress" only did Washington receive black men into his army, that the general officers resolved by a large majority that negroes of every description should be excluded, and that Congress, composed of the ablest statesmen in America, passed a law that no negroes should be received into the army as soldiers except those who had served faithfully at Cambridge. Yet it is now boldly asserted that "Washington did not hesitate to solicit the military services of negroes—that our fathers did not hesitate to put arms into the hands of the black race—that General Lafayette was not ashamed to fight beside a black soldier, and that this war will never end until the American people accept the negro race as their equals and their brothers."

The history of the campaign before Boston is a history of successive exertions to surmount almost insuperable obstacles, by one who was solicitous in the extreme to perform some great and useful achievement; and he writes, "To be restrained in every military operation for want of means to carry it on is not very pleasing, especially as the means used to conceal my weakness from the enemy conceals it also from our friends and adds to their wonder."

The other instance mentioned in the history of the war of the Revolution of the acceptance of black men into the army, was as follows. Mr. Sparks says: "In raising recruits, the plan recommended by Congress was that each State should be divided into districts, and a person be appointed to raise recruits in each, the whole to be under the direction of the State authorities. General Varnum suggested that a battalion of negroes might be raised in Rhode Island. The idea was communicated to Governor Cooke, who laid the subject before the Assembly. He reported the following result to Washington: 'Liberty is given to every effective slave to enter into the service during the war, and upon his passing muster he is absolutely made free, and entitled to all the wages, bounties and encouragements given by Congress to any soldier enlisting into the service. The masters are allowed at the rate of one hundred and twenty pounds for the most valuable slave, and in proportion for those of less value. The number of slaves in the State is not great, but it is generally thought that three hundred and upwards will be enlisted.' The report of the Assembly gives also the reasons for consenting to the enlistment of negroes. It says: 'The enemy with a great force have taken possession of the capital and a great part of this State, and this State is obliged to raise a very considerable number of troops for its own immediate defence, whereby it is, in a manner, rendered impossible to furnish recruits without adopting this measure.'"

These incidents all go to prove that under the most pressing circumstances only did our revolutionary fathers accept the military services of the negroes, who were held as property by the northern as well as southern colonies at the time of the Revolution, and were valued at as high a sum in Rhode Island as in the slave States generally since that day.

Another "crisis of distress" occurred during the war, in which it was proposed to arm the slaves. Marshall, in his Life of Washington, says:

"General Greene was informed that large reinforcements were expected by the British Army at Charleston, South Carolina, which excited great alarm, as the time of service of many of his troops was about expiring. He therefore recommended to the Governor of that State, that his army should be recruited from the slaves. The Governor laid the matter before the Legislature, which was soon afterward convened, but the measure was not adopted.

"But in the revolutionary army, however, there were many slaves attending on the officers, because slavery at that time existed in all the colonies, and there are numerous instances on record of heroic deeds performed by individual slaves, suddenly and on their own responsibility."

It is thus clearly established that our ancestors, the Patriot Fathers of the present generation in America, had no companionship or affiliation with the negro, and never adopted him into their society; that the Puritan Fathers of New England recognized no equality or brotherhood between themselves and the black race, other than is now recognized by the people who still hold them in servitude; that Massachusetts as well as South Carolina refused to arm her slaves to fight an enemy at her own door, and that the whole American people chose to fight their battles for independence without the aid of the African race.

Their independence achieved, they constructed the

best government ever devised by man—a government declared to be ordained and approved of God; and this great system was planned and devised without the aid of either the African or the Indian race. No negro or Indian ever sat in the councils of the nation, with the Fathers of the American Republic, and no counsel or advice was ever asked or received of a single member of either tribe. The nation was founded and builded up, without including within its structure either of these races of men, except in the representation of slaves. It has been said that God sifted the nations of the old world, to get the precious seed to sow a nation in the new world! But God selected that precious seed from the Caucasian race alone. The government established, the negro and Indian were alike excluded from all participation in the administration thereof. White men alone were to be its officers, and white men alone the soldiers that were to compose its future armies, the laws expressly confining the militia of the nation to white men. Wendell Phillips said in 1862: " What cripples General McClellan to-day is, that his fathers in 1789 bound one of his hands, and left him only one to fight with." When Washington fought for liberty, one-third of the American people loved the Government of Great Britain better than that founded by our fathers. That portion of the people hold the reins of government to-day. They have wickedly broken the bonds with which our fathers bound them, and have reinstated the king upon the throne from which Washington was eight long years in displacing him. They have re-asserted the divine right of kings to rule, and have re-established a regal authority over the people of America. Washington broke the yoke of George the Third from off the necks of the people. It is now replaced by a heavier one called military despotism, and a military despot sits to-day virtually crowned and enthroned in the chair of State, where, for eight happy years to America, sat the Father of his Country.

Washington addressed his soldiers soon after the arrival of General Howe, the British officer, in the following language:

"The time is now near at hand which must determine whether Americans are to be freemen or slaves; whether they are to have any property they can call their own; whether their houses and farms are to be pillaged and destroyed, and themselves consigned to a state of wretchedness, from which no human efforts will deliver them. Our cruel and unrelenting enemy leaves us only the choice of a brave resistance or the most abject submission. We have therefore to resolve to conquer or die. Let us then rely upon the goodness of our cause and the aid of the Supreme Being, in whose hands victory is, to animate and encourage us to great and noble actions. The eyes of all our countrymen are upon us, and we shall have their blessings and their praises, if happily we are the instruments of saving them from the tyranny meditated against them. Let us therefore animate and encourage each other, and show the whole world that a freeman contending for liberty on his own ground is superior to any slavish mercenary on earth. Remember that liberty, property, life and honor are all at stake."

WASHINGTON PRAYING FOR HIS COUNTRY.

"A man related to me the following incident: When the British troops held possession of New York and the

American army lay near West Point, one morning at sunrise I went forth to bring home my cows. On passing a clump of trees I heard a moaning sound, like a person in distress. On nearing the spot I heard the words of a man at prayer. I listened behind a tree. The man came forth: it was George Washington, the Captain of the Lord's hosts in North America. This man was a member of the Society of Friends, who, being opposed to war on any pretext, were lukewarm, and in some instances opposed to the cause of the country. He was a tory however. Having seen the General enter the camp he went to his house. 'Martha,' said he to his wife, 'we must not oppose this war any longer. This morning I heard the man, George Washington, send up a prayer to Heaven for his country, and I know it will be heard.' We may thus infer that Washington rose with the sun to pray for his country; he fought for her at meridian, and watched for her in the silent hours of night. This incident should be published on every 22d of February, Washington's birth-day, while wood grows and water runs."—*Grant Thornburn.*

The government, called the United States, is declared to be the best that was ever established on earth—one which was blest of God above all other nations that had an existence before it; and this government was one in which the African race had no more share than if they had never had existence upon our globe. It is therefore a manifest truth, that if God was with Washington and our fathers through the Revolution, and imparted unto them wisdom and foresight in the construction of the American Union, it was his will and pleasure that the negro was thus omitted from a place among the white people of the nation, and retained in the sphere

which had been assigned him by the English government more than a hundred years before the United
States came into existence. Washington achieved the
liberties of the white people and was called the "Father
of his Country." As Abraham was the father of the
Jewish nation, and not of the Canaanites or the Amele-
kites, so Washington was the father of the European
race in America, and not of the African or the Indian.
But God is the father of all the races of men, and when
our fathers, who were the descendants of Japheth, founded
a government in the New World, God enlarged Japheth,
and Canaan remained his servant. "A servant shall he
be to his brethren." A brother truly but a servant also.

It is declared by some that our fathers deprived the
negroes of their natural rights. But our fathers were
under the government of England until they established
their independence, and England conferred no rights
upon the negroes but the rights of the slave. Our
fathers took away no rights from them when they
founded a government of their own. They were slaves
under the English laws before our patriot fathers were
born, and their condition remained unchanged under the
government of the United States. They were slaves
in Africa before America was discovered by the European race, and would have remained in a worse state of
bondage had they never been brought to our shores.
Neither were the fathers of this Republic responsible
for negro slavery after their government was founded.
Bancroft says: "The system of slavery was fastened
upon the rising institutions of America, not by consent
of the corporation, nor the desires of the colonists, but
was riveted by the policy of England without regard to
the wishes of the people." And this institution was

fastened by the strong hand of destiny, or of Providence, and Abraham Lincoln acknowledged in September, 1860, that very truth. He says: "When Southern
people tell us they are no more responsible for the origin
of slavery than we are I acknowledge the fact. When
it is said that the institution exists, and that it is very
difficult to get rid of it in any satisfactory way, I can
understand and appreciate the saying. I surely will not
blame them for not doing what I should not know how
to do myself. If all earthly power were given me I
should not know what to do as to the existing institution." If, then, so good and wise and great a statesman
as the people believe Mr. Lincoln to be, would not know
what to do with the institution of slavery, surely the
people of the South are not to be blamed for not being
wiser than he. He says again: "When our government was established we had the institution of slavery
among us. We were in a certain sense compelled to
tolerate it. It was a sort of necessity. We had gone
through our struggle and secured our own independence.
The framers of the Constitution found the institution
among their other institutions at the time. They found
that by an effort to eradicate it they might lose much
of what they had already gained. They were obliged
to bow to the necessity; and I say that we must not
interfere with the institution of slavery in the States
where it exists, because the Constitution forbids it.
Let me say I have no prejudice against the Southern
people. They are just what we would be in their situation. If slavery did not exist among them, they would
not introduce it. If it did now exist among us, we
should not instantly give it up. We know that some
Southern men do free their slaves, while some Northern

ones go South and become most cruel slave-masters. I will say here that I have no purpose, directly or indirectly, to interfere with the institution of slavery in the States where it exists. I believe I have no lawful right to do so, and I have no inclination to do so. I will say that I have no purpose to introduce political and social equality between the white and the black races, that I am not, and never have been in favor of making voters or jurors of negroes, nor of qualifying them to hold office, nor to intermarry with white people, and I will say in addition to this, that there is a physical difference between the white and black races, which will, I believe, forever forbid the two races living together on terms of social and political equality. And inasmuch as they cannot so live, while they do remain together, there must be the position of superior and inferior, and I, as much as any other man, am in favor of having the superior position assigned to the white race."

Abbott, in his history of Alfred the Great, says:

" Physiologists consider that there are five great races of men, whose characteristics, mental as well as bodily, are distinctly, strongly, and permanently marked; and though education and outward influence may modify them, they cannot essentially change them. Compare, for example, the Indian and the African races. How entirely diverse from each other they are, not only in form, color, and other physical marks, but in all the tendencies and characteristics of the soul. The difference is still greater between these and the Caucasian race. This race may be properly called the European race. That there have been some noble specimens of humanity among the African race, none can deny; but that there is a fixed and constitutional difference between them and the Caucasian race is evident from the fact, that for two thousand years each has held its own continent undisturbed in a great degree by the rest of mankind; and while, during all this time, no nation of the African race has risen, so far as is known, above the lowest stage of civilization, there have been more than fifty entirely distinct and independent civilizations originated and fully developed in the other. For three thousand years the Caucasian race have continued in all circumstances, and every variety of situation, to exhibit the same traits and the same indomitable power. No calamities, however great, no desolation, no night of darkness, however gloomy, have been able to keep them long in a state of barbarism. As Egyptians, they built the pyramids; as Phœnicians, they constructed ships and perfected navigation; as Greeks, they modelled architecture, cut sculptures in marble, wrote poems and history; as Romans, they commanded a perfect military organization over fifty nations, and a hundred millions of people." "These are the descendants of Japheth."

In 1830, Gerrit Smith says: "Look at Africa! What contribution has she brought for the last thousand years to the arts or the sciences? Has a single valuable book been printed during that long period in Africa? Her moral and intellectual state is more cheerless than her deserts—her mind is a total waste, presenting a desolation without one redeeming feature. Her barbarism has rendered her soil almost as useless as if the ocean had been permitted to roll over it."

On February 22d, 1862, the Chaplain of Congress, Rev. Mr. Stockton, offered up the following prayer in the capitol of our nation:

"Oh Lord, blessed be thy name for the supreme

foresight which gave Moses to Israel and Washington to America. Blessed be thy name for the birth, life, character, accomplishments, and achievements of the model man, and patriot soldier, and magistrate, whom we this day remember, not only as first in war, first in peace, and first in the hearts of his countrymen, but also as first in the veneration and admiration of mankind. Blessed be thy name that Washington was a man of prayer, that he called upon thee, that he trusted in Christ, and that in accepting office, filling office, resigning office, he called on thee, commending himself to thy favor and beseeching thy blessing."

And this Moses of America, this model man, this man of prayer, this Christian, who trusted in Christ, who commended himself to the favor of God, was a slaveholder, and an owner of slaves. Bancroft says: "Abraham, the founder of the Jewish nation, was a slaveholder, and a purchaser of slaves. Every patriarch was lord of his own household." So the patriarchs of America were slaveholders as well as the "Father of his Country." Washington Irving, in his life of the illustrious founder of the nation, describes the households of the patriarchs as follows:

"A large Virginia estate was a little empire. The mansion house was the seat of government, and in this mansion the planter reigned supreme. He had his legions of negroes for domestic service, and hosts of others for the culture of the land. They had a kind of hamlet apart, with little gardens, and poultry yards, well stocked. Among the slaves were artificers of all kinds, tailors, shoemakers, carpenters, smiths, wheelwrights, etc., so that a plantation produced every thing within itself, for ordinary use: as to articles of fashion and elegance,

2

luxuries, and expensive clothing, they were imported from London, for the planters on the rivers, especially on the Potomac, carried on an immediate trade with England."

Howard Malcolm, in his Bible Dictionary, says : " The Hebrews had several kinds of servants, viz.: the slaves for life, and Hebrew or bond servants, who could only at the first be bound for six years. Slavery was common before the flood, and some of the patriarchs, as Job and Abraham, appear to have owned thousands, though they seem to have been treated with great tenderness, and often to have had wages and high character."

And history testifies to the kindness with which Washington, Jefferson, and the other patriarchs of our country treated their slaves; and Washington, though not a father, was a kind master to his African servants.

Irving says: "Washington treated his negroes with kindness, attended to their comforts, was particularly careful of them in sickness, but never tolerated idleness, and exacted a faithful performance of all their allotted tasks. He provided in his will for the freedom of his slaves upon the death of his wife."

Achille Murat, in his Sketch of the United States, relates the following incident: " The writer of this article was once rambling over the estate of Mount Vernon, in Virginia, formerly the property of General Washington, and having lost his way, entered into conversation with an old negress, who had formerly been a slave on the estate, but had been free six years. She concluded the conversation by wishing that she were a slave still, for in that state she had nothing to think of, whereas, being free, she could *hardly make a living*."

In 1793, Washington wrote to Arthur Young, as follows:

" SIR—All my landed property east of the Appalachian mountains is under rent, except the estate called Mount Vernon. This hitherto I have kept in my own hands, but from my advanced time of life, from a wish to live from care during the remainder of it, I have thought of letting this estate also, reserving the Mansion House Farm for my own residence, occupation and amusement in agriculture. There are four farms, besides that of the Mansion House. These four farms contain three thousand two hundred and sixty acres of cultivated land. On Union farm there is a brick house, and a new house is now building; convenient thereto is sufficient accommodation for fifty odd negroes, old and young, but these buildings might not be thought good enough for the workmen of your country. Dague farm has covering for forty odd negroes, Muddy Hole farm has covering for thirty negroes, River farm, the largest of the four, has sufficient covering for fifty or sixty negroes.

" GEORGE WASHINGTON."

While Washington was fighting for his country his plantation was left to the ravages of the enemy. In 1781, he wrote to Lund Washington, at Mount Vernon, as follows:

" NEW WINDSOR, 30th April, 1781.

" DEAR LUND—I am very sorry for your loss. I am a little sorry for my own, but that which gives me most concern is, that you should go on board the enemy's vessels, and furnish them with refreshments. It would have been a less painful circumstance to me, to have heard, that in consequence of your non-compliance with their request they had burnt my house, and laid my plantation in ruins. I am persuaded you acted from your best judgment, and believe that your desire to preserve my property, and rescue the buildings from impending danger of conflagration, was your governing motive, but to go on board their vessels, carry them refreshments, and request a favor by asking a surrender of my negroes, was exceedingly ill-judged. I have no doubt of the enemy's intention to prosecute the plundering plan they have begun, and unless a stop can be put to it, by the arrival of superior force, I have as little doubt of its ending in a loss of all my negroes, and in the destruction of my houses, but I am prepared for the event, under the prospect of which, if you could deposit in a place of safety the most valuable articles, it might be consistent with policy and prudence." It was the strong desire of. the people of Virginia, that Washington should take command of the army in that State. Writing upon the subject, he said : " Nobody, I am persuaded, can doubt my inclination to be immediately employed in the defence of that country where all my property and connections are, but there are powerful objections to my leaving this army. One only will I name, which is, that no other person has power to command the French troops, who are now about to form a junction with this army. Let it suffice for me to add, that I am acting on a great scale, that temporary evils must be endured, and that I am not without hope that the tables may be turned.

" GEORGE WASHINGTON."

" The Father of his Country" calls his African slaves " my negroes." What equality existed between Washington and his negroes? The distance between them was as great as it is possible for human beings to be separated from each other in rank and condition of life. He was of the highest type of the European race—they his abject slaves—and yet no man can say that Washington degraded these members of the human family, and reduced them to that humble place beside him. Both were born to the station in which we find them. Washington inherited these negroes from his ancestors. His ancestors purchased them from the English merchants, who bought them of those who held them as slaves in Africa. Could they have looked into the wretched country from whence they came, they would have rejoiced that Providence ordered their birth in the country of Washington, that he was their master instead of the king of Dahomey or Ashantee, or any other king or chief on the whole African continent, and thus would the millions now in servitude rejoice were they to behold their brethren in the land of barbarism and death.

At a meeting of the Missionary Board in New York, May, 1860, Rev. Daniel Lord, of South Africa, said he had a home 1200 miles beyond the Cape of Good Hope, and ten miles inland, from which he could see the commerce of the world going to and fro on the Indian Ocean. To the west he looked through thousands of miles of unbroken heathenism. Though these vessels had been sailing over that track for 300 years, yet he had talked with thousands who, for the first time, had ever heard the name of Jesus. He had heard this week men talk of the rights of humanity. That was good: liberty for four millions of men in bondage. God give them liberty, but God give liberty to 150,000,000 of their brethren in that land from which they were brought. These people were so barbarous that if a woman had two children at a time, one of them was killed because she could not do her work with the two. Contrast the heathen in Africa to the Christian. He knew a young man who gave all that he had to buy his sister out of slavery in Africa. The heathen African slept on the ground in their huts between the sheep and the calves." The people in Africa worship reptiles. They have a large-house for the snakes. The missionary peeped in and saw hundreds of them. They are fed by the natives with fowls and milk. Sometimes, when pressed by hunger, they go into the huts of the natives. Not a great while ago, a huge boa entered a hut and seized a poor infant which was playing on the floor. The mother rushed in at the cry, and beheld it wrapped in the fatal coil; but it was her god who embraced it, and she could only beseech him not to eat her child till it was quite dead. A missionary, Rev. Joel Parker, said a few years ago: " The Africans were first taken from a home where they had been degraded by the bondage of many centuries. They were brought hither, not to a heavier bondage, but to a lighter one, for American slavery is more tolerable than African slavery. So that if you take 10,000 born here in slavery and compare them with 10,000 born there, the comparison is in favor of the American slave. Men have endeavored to prove that the holding of a slave is evidence of guilt. The effort has failed. The word of God is not bound. False interpretations cannot gain general credence, and the American people will never be convinced by the seeming of logic that thousands of our slaveholding brethren are not excellent, humane, and even Christian men, fearing God and keeping his commandments."

And yet the American people North have been convinced by infidels, who reject the Bible altogether, that to hold a negro in slavery is a sin of the deepest dye.

In 1783, Washington wrote to Sir Guy Carleton, as follows:

"Sir—In my letter of April 4, I enclosed to your excellency a copy of resolutions of Congress, instructing me in three points, which appeared necessary to carry into effect the terms of the treaty between Great Britain and the United States, respecting the carrying away of any negroes or other property of the people. I was surprised to hear that an embarkation had already taken place, in which a large number of negroes had been taken away. I cannot conceal from you that my private opinion is, that the measure is totally different from the letter and spirit of the treaty, but leaving the decision to our respective sovereigns, I find it my duty to signify my readiness to take any measures which may be expedient to prevent the future carrying away of any negroes or other property of the American people.

"GEORGE WASHINGTON."

In 1791, he wrote to James Seagrove, Collector of the Port at St. Mary's, as follows:

"Sir—The confidence which your character inclines me to place in you has induced me to commit to your care the enclosed letter from the Secretary of State to Governor Quesada [Spanish Governor], and the negotiation consequent thereon. Your first care will be to arrest the farther reception of fugitive slaves; your next, to obtain restitution of those slaves who have fled to Florida, and to procure the Governor's orders for the general relinquishment of all fugitive slaves who were the property of citizens of the United States.

"GEORGE WASHINGTON."

Here is proof that Washington considered slaves as the property of the American people.

In his debates with the immortal Douglas, Abraham Lincoln said: "An inspection of the Constitution will show that the right of property in a slave is not distinctly and expressly affirmed in it. Neither the word slave, or slavery, is to be found in the Constitution, nor the word property, even in any connection with language alluding to the things slave or slavery, and, wherever in that instrument the slave is alluded to, he is called a person, and this mode of alluding to slaves was employed on purpose to exclude from the Constitution the idea that there could be property in man."

Now what a delusion the Republican leaders threw over the minds of the American people! In the Life of John Adams, one of the signers of the "Declaration," by his grandson, Charles F. Adams, it is said:

"In the plans formed for the first Confederation, a question touched the proper apportionment of the public charges. The plan adopted was to base it exclusively on land and buildings. New England would have it extended to other property, included in the term African slaves. The other States, in which this description of population was mostly found, preferred then, to except themselves from charge, by considering them exclusively as persons. This distinction should always be borne in mind in connection with the language of the Constitution, framed eleven years afterwards."

There, Mr. Lincoln, you have the reason why slaves are called persons, instead of property. After the Constitution was formed, it was submitted to all the States for their adoption. While they were examining and considering its merits, James Madison, Alexander Hamilton, and John Jay, wrote an explanation of every Article, and published their expositions in a paper called "The Federalist." In this paper is found the following, by James Madison:

"Slaves are considered by some as property, and not as persons. They ought, therefore, to be comprehended in estimates of taxation which are founded on property, and to be excluded from representation which is regulated by a census of persons. The true state of the case is, they partake of both these qualities, being considered by our laws, in some respects, as persons, and in other respects, as property. The Federal Constitution decides with great propriety on the case of our slaves, when it views them in the mixed character of persons and of property. This is, in fact, their true character. May not some surprise be expressed that those who reproach the Southern States with the barbarous policy of considering as property a part of their human brethren, should themselves contend that the government ought to consider this unfortunate race more completely in the light of property than the very laws of the South, of which they complain?"

James Madison has been quoted as saying there could be no such thing as property in man. In the Virginia debates upon the adoption of the Constitution he remarks: "One clause secures us that property we now possess. It says, 'No person held to service or labor in one State under the laws thereof, escaping into another, shall, in consequence of any law or regulation thereof, be discharged from such service or labor; but shall be delivered up on claim of the party to whom such service or labor is due.'" This clause was expressly inserted, to enable owners of slaves to reclaim them.

No power is given to the general government to interpose with respect to property in slaves now held by the States. Thus did Madison endeavor to bring his State into the Union, by assuring the people that the government would never interpose with respect to property in slaves. Better for Virginia, and the other Southern States, had they remained separate and independent, than to have had the Government fallen into the hands of Abraham Lincoln and the Abolitionists, now desolating their soil!

Patrick Henry, the great Virginia patriot, who declaimed against Great Britain, and ended an eloquent speech with the oft-repeated sentence, "As for me, give me liberty or give me death!" said in this convention, "As much as I deplore slavery, I see that prudence forbids its abolition. I repeat that it would rejoice my very soul that every one of my fellow-beings was emancipated. But is it practicable, by any human means, to liberate them without producing the most dreadful consequences? We ought to possess them in the manner we inherited them from our ancestors, as their manumission is incompatible with the felicity of our country. But we ought to soften, as much as possible, the rigor of their unhappy fate. I wish this property, therefore, to be guarded." Such was the decision of Patrick Henry, when it was suggested to the people of Virginia that the general government, if they should consent to come into a Union with the North, might attempt to emancipate their slaves. He says, " This property, as well as every other property of the people of Virginia, is in jeopardy, and put in the hands of those who have no similarity of situation with us." How fearful, how sensitive, how apprehensive of danger, were the people of Virginia, that the Eastern States would take advantage if they put themselves in their power. Another gentleman, Mr. Galloway, asked, "If we must manumit our slaves, what country shall we send them to? It is impossible for us to be happy if, after manumission, they are to stay among us." This harmonizes with Thomas Jefferson's belief that the two races could not live under the same government equally free.

In the North Carolina debates it was said by Mr. Davie that the Eastern States had great jealousies on the subject of representation. They insisted that their horses and cows were equally entitled to representation as the negroes—that the one was property as well as the other. In South Carolina, Hon. Mr. Lowndes said: "It has been remarked that this new government was to be considered as an experiment. He really was afraid it would prove a fatal one to our peace and happiness. An experiment! what? risk the loss of political existence on experiments? So far from having any expectation of success from such an experiment he believed that when this new Constitution should be adopted, the sun of the Southern States would set, never to rise again. To prove this, he said that six of the Eastern States formed a majority in the House of Representatives. Now, was it consonant with reason, with wisdom, with policy, to suppose, in a legislature, where a majority of persons sat whose interests were greatly different from ours, that we had the smallest chance of receiving adequate advantages? Certainly not. The Eastern States drew their means of subsistence, in a great measure, from their shipping; and on that head they had been particularly careful not to allow of any burdens; they were not to pay tonnage or duties, no, not even the form of clearing out; all ports were free and open to them. Why then call this a reciprocal bargain, which took all from one party to bestow it on the other? They don't like our slaves, because they have so few themselves, and therefore want to exclude us from this great advantage. The nature of our climate, and the flat, swampy situation of our country obliges us to cultivate our lands with negroes, and without them South Carolina would soon be a desert waste."

General Pinckney decided the question by telling the people that the "general government could never emancipate our negroes, for no such authority is granted, as the general government has no powers but what are expressly granted by the Constitution, and all rights not expressed are reserved by the several States."

And thus assured, the hitherto free, sovereign, and independent States, south of the Potomac, united in a bond of union with the sovereign and independent States north and east, on the great continent of America.

On the 8th of June, 1783, Washington addressed to the Governors of the several States the paternal and affectionate letter which follows:

" The citizens of America, placed in the most enviable condition as the sole lords and proprietors of a vast tract of continent, comprehending all the various soils and climates of the world, and abounding with all the necessaries and conveniences of life, are now, by the late satisfactory pacification, acknowledged to be possessed of absolute freedom and independence. They are from this period to be considered as the actors on a most conspicuous theatre, which seems to be peculiarly designated by Providence for the display of human greatness

and felicity. Here they are not only surrounded with
every thing which can contribute to the completion of
private and domestic enjoyment, but heaven has crowned
all its other blessings by giving a fairer opportunity for
political happiness than any other nation has been
favored with. Nothing can illustrate these observations
more forcibly than a recollection of the happy conjunc-
ture of times and circumstances under which our republic
assumed its rank among the nations.

"The foundation of our empire was not laid in the
gloomy age of ignorance and superstition, but at an
epoch when the rights of mankind were better understood and more clearly defined, than at any former
period. The researches of the human mind after social
happiness have been carried to a great extent, the
treasures of knowledge acquired by the labors of philosophers, sages, and legislators, through a long succession
of years, are laid open to our use, and their collected
wisdom may be happily employed in the establishment
of our forms of government. The free cultivation of
letters, and above all, the pure and benign light of revelation, have had a meliorating influence on mankind and
increased the blessings of society. At this auspicious
period the United States came into existence as a nation,
and if their citizens should not be completely free and
happy, the fault will be entirely their own."

To those who say that our fathers lived in a barbarous
age, the above is an answer. The treasures of knowledge acquired by all the Grecian and Roman legislators
and philosophers were laid open for their use; and, above
all, the Bible was theirs, and there is but one revelation
from God to man. If the citizens of the United States were
not happy the fault was indeed their own. The nation

prospered as our fathers made it. It rose to the highest rank among the nations of the earth, and would have continued to prosper had it not been for the causes set forth in the following pages.

As Moses gave laws to Israel, so Washington gave laws to America. He made, with the assistance of the ablest in the land, a Constitution or code of laws for the government of the people, and, with the other laws, there were those with regard to slavery. As the founders of the Christian religion taught both by precept and example, so did the founders of the American republic. To those States which had dispensed with negro slavery, it was said:

"Thou shalt not entice a slave to leave his master, and shall restore to his owner the fugitive who may escape unto thee. Thou shalt not excite them to insurrection, but shall aid in suppressing all rising of the slaves."

And Washington said: "I now make it my most earnest prayer that God would incline the hearts of the citizens to cultivate a spirit of subordination and obedience to government, to entertain a brotherly affection and love for one another, for their fellow-citizens of the United States at large; that he would most graciously be pleased to dispose us all to do justice, to love mercy and to demean ourselves with that charity, humility, and pacific temper of mind which were the characteristics of the Divine Author of our blessed religion, without an humble imitation of whose example in these things we can never hope to be a happy nation."

" The Lord spake to Moses, and said: 'Say unto the people of Israel, if ye walk in my statutes, and keep my commandments to do them, I will give peace in the land, and ye shall lie down, and none shall make you afraid, neither shall the sword go through your land. But if ye will not hearken unto me, and will not do all my commandments, ye shall perish among the heathen, and the land of your enemies shall eat you up, and they that are left of you shall pine away in their iniquity in your enemies' land. Behold, I set before you, this day, life and death, a blessing and a curse."

The sword has gone through our land, and thousands have pined away in our enemies' country: a curse has come upon us—the curse of war and bloodshed. Who are the people that have broken the commands of Washington, and the laws of our fathers? Is the wickedness all on the side of the people against whom our government is sending forth war and desolation? Let the facts of history answer.

In March, 1790, General Washington received the following letter from Dr. Stuart of Virginia:

"DEAR SIR—A spirit of jealousy, which may become dangerous to the Union, seems to be growing fast among us. Colonel Lee tells me that many who were strong supporters of the government are changing their sentiments, from a conviction of impracticability of union with States whose interests are so dissimilar to those of Virginia. The late application to Congress respecting slaves will certainly tend to promote this spirit. It gives particular umbrage that the Quakers should be so busy in this matter."

Washington answered the letter and endeavored to reconcile the people of Virginia, by telling them that "The memorial of the Quakers, and a very *mal apropos* one it was, had at length been put to sleep, and would scarcely awake before the year 1808."

Daniel Webster, in speaking of this subject, says: "When the present Constitution of the United States was submitted for the ratification of the people, there were some who imagined that the powers of the new government might, perhaps, in some possible mode, be exerted in measures tending to the abolition of slavery. This suggestion attracted much attention in the Southern Conventions. At the very first Congress petitions were presented praying Congress to abolish slavery. The House of Representatives referred these petitions to a select committee, consisting of Mr. Foster of New Hampshire, Mr. Gerry of Massachusetts, Mr. Huntington of Connecticut, Mr. Lawrence of New York, Mr. Sinnickson of New Jersey, Mr. Hartley of Pennsylvania, and Mr. Parker of Virginia, all of them Northern men but the last. This committee made a report as follows: 'Resolved, That Congress have no authority to interfere in the emancipation of slaves, or in the treatment of them in any of the States, it remaining with the several States alone to provide rules and regulations therein, which humanity and true policy may require.'

"This resolution received the sanction of Congress as early as March, 1790, and they agreed to insert the resolutions in their journals; and from that day to this (1830) it has never been maintained or contended that Congress had any authority to interfere with the condition of slaves in the several States. The fears of the South, whatever fears they might have entertained, were allayed and quieted by this early decision."

General Washington wrote to the Governor of Rhode Island as soon as that State and North Carolina accepted the Constitution, and joined the other States. "Since the bond of Union is now complete, and we once more

consider ourselves as one family, it is hoped that re-
proaches will cease, and prejudices be done away, for if
we mean to support the liberty and independence which
has cost us so much blood and treasure, we must drive
away the demon of party spirit and local reproach.
The introduction of the Quaker memorial was not only
ill timed but occasioned a great waste of time."

The local reproach means the same as that used by
Madison when he speaks of those who reproach the
South for slavery. Washington's whole aim and ambition was to have his family of white children, North and
South, live in happiness and peace together in the Union
which was now completed. Since we once more consider ourselves as one family, if we mean to retain our
liberty and independence, we must drive away the
demon of party spirit, and not reproach one another—
"frowning upon every attempt to alienate any portion
of our country from the rest."

When the petitions were sent to the first Congress
praying for the abolition of slavery, Mr. Smith, a member from the South, made a speech, of which the following is an extract: "The Southern people might consider
the toleration of the Quakers an injury to the community,
because in time of war they would not defend their
country from the enemy, and in time of peace they
were doing all in their power to excite the slaves in
the Southern States to insurrection; notwithstanding
which the people of these States have not required the
assistance of Congress to exterminate the Quakers.
The Northern States knew the Southern States had
slaves before they confederated with them. If they had
such an abhorrence of slavery, why did they not reject
our alliance? The truth was, that the best informed

3

citizens of the North knew that slavery was so ingrafted into the policy of the Southern States, that it could not be eradicated without tearing up by the roots their happiness and prosperity—that if it were an evil, it was one for which there was no remedy, and, therefore, like wise men, they acquiesced in it. We, therefore, made a compromise on both sides; we took each other with our mutual bad habits and respective evils for better or worse; the Northern States adopted us with our slaves, and we adopted them with their Quakers. There was then an implied contract between the Northern and Southern people that no step should be taken to injure the property of the Southern people or to disturb their tranquillity."

The Hon. Mr. Charles Diven, M.C., explains this contract more fully in a speech upon the Personal Liberty Bill attempted to be passed in the Legislature of New York. He says:

"The Constitution is in the nature of compact between independent States, by which a government was created for specific purposes, mutually beneficial; but was confined in its powers to these specific purposes. In all other respects the States retained their sovereignty. No one State was to become responsible for the laws of another; we have no right to make laws for South Carolina, consequently we are in no respect responsible for her laws, nor has she any right to make laws for us. Will it be said that she has no right to complain if we pass this law? The answer is, that by the compact we expressly agreed not to pass such laws: we agreed solemnly that we should respect this law of hers, by which she recognized this right in slaves. These laws existed at the time of the compact, with a perfect knowledge of their existence. The South held slaves without a Union. The Union did not give them this power. Is the State of New York prepared to break the compact, as it certainly will by the passage of this bill?"

A great many Northern States passed the Personal Liberty Bill: therefore the Northern people broke the compact that held the Union together long before the South seceded. All who favored such a bill broke the commands of the Father of his Country. They violated the national compact, and trod under their feet the Constitution which Washington signed his name to, when first elected President of the United States. In 1789, he made an inaugural address, in which he says:

"No people can be bound to acknowledge and adore the invisible hand which conducts the affairs of men, more than the people of the United States. Every step by which they have advanced to the character of an independent nation, seems to have been distinguished by some token of Providential agency. There is no truth more firmly established than that there exists, in the course and economy of nature, an indissoluble union between virtue and happiness, and I behold in the characters selected to adopt the measures of government, which it is made the duty of the President to recommend, the surest pledges that the foundation of our policy will be laid in the pure and immutable principles of private morality, and the pre-eminence of free government be exemplified by all the attributes which can win the affections of the citizens, and command the respect of the world. We ought to be persuaded that the propitious smiles of heaven can never be expected on a nation that disregards the eternal rules of order and right which Heaven itself has ordained."

> " Order is Heaven's first law, and this confest,
> Some are, and must be, greater than the rest."

These " eternal rules of order and right" Washington illustrated both by precept and example. An illustration of his principles, and his ideas of justice and order, may be found in the following letter to Robert Morris, of Philadelphia, April, 1786:

"DEAR SIR—I give you the trouble of this letter at the instance of Mr. Dalby, of Alexandria, who is called to Philadelphia to attend what he conceives to be a vexatious lawsuit, respecting a slave of his, whom a society of Quakers in the city, formed for such purposes, have attempted to liberate. From Mr. Dalby's statement of the matter, it should seem that this society is not only acting repugnantly to justice, so far as its conduct concerns strangers, but in my opinion impolitically with respect to the State, the city in particular, without being able, except by acts of tyranny and oppression, to accomplish its own ends. He says the conduct of this society is not sanctioned by law. Had the case been otherwise, whatever my opinion of the law might have been, my respect for the policy of the State would, on this occasion, have appeared in my silence, because, against the penalty of promulgated laws, one may guard; but there is no avoiding the snares of individuals or private societies. If the practice of this society is not discountenanced, none of those whose misfortune it is to have slaves as attendants, will visit the city if they can possibly avoid it, because, by so doing, they hazard their property, or they must be at the expense (and this will not always succeed) of providing servants of another description."

Here the Father of his Country places an emphatic condemnation on all societies or persons who would entice a slave from his master. He pronounces their acts repugnant to justice, and says that it is only by tyranny and oppression they gain the liberty of the slave, which he calls the property of his master. Now, it is their acts of tyranny that constitute men and rulers tyrants— by their acts of oppression that they are called oppressors. Then what a band of tyrants and oppressors have been formed in the Northern States to steal away the property of their white brethren South! Thirty thousand slaves in Canada alone have been stolen or enticed from Southern people by Northern abolitionists—a great gang of negro-stealers, whom Washington himself pronounced guilty of tyranny and oppression, holding themselves up before the world as models of justice and philanthropy, and denouncing slaveholders as the worst of men. Washington says: "When slaves who are happy and contented with their present masters, are tampered with, and seduced to leave them, when masters are taken unawares by these practices, when a conduct of this kind begets discontent on one side, and resentment on the other, and when it happens to fall on a man whose purse will not measure with that of the society, and he loses his property for want of means to defend it, it is oppression in such a case, and not humanity in any, because it introduces more evils than it can cure."

He says it is oppression to seduce away slaves from their masters, who have not the means of defending their property, even when they are not happy and contented. It seems Washington thought there were contented and happy slaves; but even when they were unhappy it was not humanity to take them from their masters, because it would introduce more evils than it could cure. Thus we have the testimony of the Father of his Country, who was trying to act indeed as a father to his children, that the abolitionists have not been performing acts of humanity in any case, for that they have introduced more evils than they have cured.

Washington speaks of the acts of the society not being sanctioned by law. That was true. Thomas Benton, who published the Debates in Congress, says: "Public opinion was against the abduction of slaves, and if any one was seduced from his owner it was done furtively and secretly, as any other moral offence would be committed. State laws favored the owner, and to a greater extent than the act of Congress, called the Fugitive Slave law, did or could." In Pennsylvania there was an act passed in 1780, and only repealed in 1847, discriminating between the traveller and sojourner, and the permanent resident, allowing the former to remain six months in the State before his slaves would become subject to the emancipation laws, which are as follows:

"No man or woman of any nation or color, except the negroes and mulattoes who shall be registered as aforesaid, shall at any time hereafter be deemed adjudged or holden within the territories of this Commonwealth as slaves or servants for life, except the domestic slaves attending upon delegates in Congress from other American States, foreign ministers and consuls, and persons passing through or sojourning in this State, provided such slaves be not retained in this State longer than six months."

The slave then of Mr. Dalby was not free by coming into Pennsylvania, and up to 1847 the Southern people could travel with their slaves through the State or remain six months without losing them by law. New York had the same act, only varying in time. While these two acts were in force and supported by public opinion, the traveller and sojourner was safe with his slaves in those States, and the same in other free States.

It is a fact to be remembered, that Washington claimed the right of the Southern people to travel through the States with their slaves without running the hazard of their being enticed away by abolitionists, and when the South since claimed the same privilege they asked no more than the Father of the Country did before them.

Daniel S. Dickinson, in a speech made in 1860, said: "This Union was founded in mutual friendship and regard. In 1840, the law called the nine months law was repealed. It permitted Southern brethren, who visited the State of New York, to bring with them their servants and remain nine months, and they were as fully protected as they were in the States from whence they came. In 1840 that act was repealed. I was then a member of the Senate, and resisted the repeal of that law to the best of my ability. I believe that was the first trouble between the North and the South. The Federal laws and Constitution are well enough. The South insists upon the principle of the equality of the States, and they are entitled to it. The Constitution makes them equal; the law makes them equal; they are equals in the sight of honest men, and are equals in the sight of God, and woe be to him who undertakes to degrade them and trample them down."

While this question was being discussed two years before the law was repealed, William H. Seward made the following remarks: " Being desirous to be entirely candid in this communication, it is proper that I should add that I am not convinced it would be either wise, expedient or humane to declare to our fellow-citizens of the Southern States, that if they travel to or from, or pass through the State of New York, they shall not bring with them the attendants whom custom, or education, or habit may have rendered necessary to them. I have not been able to discover any good object to be attained by such an act of inhospitality. It certainly can work no injury to us, nor can it be injurious to the unfortunate beings held in bondage to permit them, once perhaps in their lives, and at most on occasions few and far between, to visit a country where slavery is unknown. I can even conceive of benefits to the great cause of human liberty from the cultivation of this intercourse with the South. It is sufficient to say that such an exclusion could have no good effect practically, and would accomplish nothing in the great cause of human liberty." But this act of inhospitality was passed, and all intercourse with the people of the South ended with it.

General Washington was President of the Convention that framed the Constitution, and affixed his name to that instrument which contained the Fugitive Slave Law. Daniel Webster said in regard to this, in a speech made a year before he died:

" There has been an ancient practice for a century for aught I know, according to which, fugitives from service, whether apprentices at the North or slaves at the South, should be restored. Massachusetts had restored fugitive slaves to Virginia long before the adoption of the Constitution. And it was held that any man could pursue his slave and take him wherever he could find him. Under this state of things it was expressly stipulated in the plainest language, and there it stands—sophistry cannot gloss it, it cannot be erased from the page of the Constitution—there it stands, that ' persons held to service or labor in one State, under the laws thereof, escaping into another State, shall not, in consequence of any law or regulation therein, be discharged from such service or labor, but shall be delivered up upon claim of the party to whom such service is due.' Adopted without dissent, nowhere objected to, North or South, considered as a matter of absolute right and justice to the Southern States, concurred in everywhere by every State that adopted the Constitution, we look in vain for any opposition from Massachusetts to Georgia. Then this being the case, this being the provision of the Constitution, soon after Congress had organized in General Washington's time, it was found necessary to pass a law to carry that provision of the Constitution into effect. Such a law was prepared and passed. It is said it was drawn by Mr. Cabot of Massachusetts. It was supported by him and Mr. Goodhue and Mr. Sedgwick of Massachusetts, and generally by all the free States. So it went on until some fourteen years ago, when some of the free States passed laws prohibiting their own officers and magistrates from executing this law of Congress under heavy penalties. They said, we shall not execute the laws; no runaway slave shall be restored. But here was the constitutional compact, here was the stipulation as solemn as words could form it, and which every member of Congress, every officer from Governors down to Constables, had sworn to support.

"Well, under this state of things, in 1850 I was of the opinion that common justice and good faith called upon us to make a law, fair, equitable, just, that should be calculated to carry this constitutional provision into effect, and give the Southern States what they are entitled to, and what was intended originally they should receive. It was no concession, it was yielding nothing, giving up nothing. When called upon to fulfil a compact, the question is, Will you fulfil it? The law of 1850 was more favorable for the fugitive than the law of 1793, passed under General Washington's administration. And everywhere, by all judges, it has been pronounced to be a constitutional law. So say Judge Nelson, Woodbury, and all the rest, so far as I know. So says the unanimous opinion of Massachusetts herself, expressed by as good a court as ever sat in Massachusetts, its present Supreme Court, and so says everybody eminent for learning and good judgment, without dissent of judicial opinion, everywhere.

" And yet this law is opposed, violently opposed—not by bringing the question into court. These lovers of human liberty, these friends of the slave—the fugitive slave—don't put their hands in their pockets, and draw funds to conduct lawsuits and try the question; they are not in that habit much. ' That is not the way they show their devotion to liberty of any kind. But they meet and pass resolutions, they resolve that the law is oppressive, unjust, and should not be executed at any rate. This has been said in the States of New York, Massachusetts, and Ohio over and over again. This was the language of a Convention at Worcester, in Syracuse, and elsewhere. And for this they pledged their lives, their fortunes and their sacred honor. Now, gentlemen, these proceedings, I say it upon my professional reputation, are distinctly treasonable. And the act of taking away Shadrack from the public authorities in Boston was an act of clear treason. I speak this in the hearing of men who are lawyers; I speak it out to the country; I say it everywhere on my professional reputation: it was treason and nothing else. If men get together, and combine together, and resolve that they will oppose a law of the government, not in any one case, but in all cases—I say, if they resolve to resist this law, and carry that purpose into effect by resisting the application of the law in any one case, that, sir, is treason. The resolution itself, unacted on, is not treason; it only manifests a treasonable purpose. When this purpose is proclaimed, and it is proclaimed that it will be carried into effect by force of arms—or numbers—in any one case, that constitutes a case looking to war against the Union."

Now, by the ablest lawyer in the United States, the abolitionists of the North have been pronounced either guilty of treason or of treasonable proceedings and purposes; and when the affairs of this nation come to be adjusted, they deserve the same punishment that is meted out to traitors in the Southern States, and the Almighty will hold them responsible for their share in dissolving this Union, just the same as he will the traitors South.

Joshua Giddings says in 1846: "Our people, under the Constitution, and under the law of 1793, are prohibited, first, from protecting the slave against an arrest by the master; secondly, from concealing the slave from the master; and, thirdly, from rescuing the slave after his arrest. If we do either of these acts we violate our constitutional compact."

Wayland's Science of Moral Law, upon the subject of Contracts, says:

"A contract is a mutual promise—that is, we promise to do one thing, on the condition that another person does another. Hence, after a contract is made, while the other party performs his part; we are under obligation to perform our part; but if either party fail, the other is, by the failure of the condition essential to the contract, liberated. But this is not all. Not only is the one party liberated, by the failure of the other party to perform his part of the contract; the first, has, moreover, upon the second, a claim for damages, to the amount of what he may have suffered by such failure. The obligation to veracity is precisely the same, under what relations soever it may be formed. It is as binding between individuals and society, on both parts, as it is between individuals. There is no more excuse for a society, when it violates its obligation to an individual, or for an individual, when he violates his obligation to a society, than in any other case of deliberate falsehood. By how much more are societies or communities bound to fidelity, in their engagements with each other, since the faith of treaties is the only barrier which interposes to shield nations from the appeal to bloodshed in every case of collision of interests! And the obligation is the same, under what circumstances soever nations may treat with each other. A civilized people have no right to violate its solemn obligations because the other party is uncivilized. A strong nation has no right to lie to a weak nation. The simple fact, that two communities of moral agents have entered into engagements, binds

both of them equally in the sight of their common
Creator.

" Men may mystify before each other, and they may
stupefy the monitor in their own bosoms by throwing
the blame of perfidy upon each other, but it is to be remembered that they act in the presence of a Being with
whom the night shineth as the day, and that they must
appear before a tribunal where there will be no more
shuffling."

Hon. Henry S. Hilliard, of Alabama, in a speech at
the Cooper Institute, in 1859, in reply to Hon. Wm. H.
Seward—that liberty is always right, and slavery is
always wrong—said: " Now I deny his authority as a
statesman to frame any such proposition. I deny his
authority to engraft an anti-slavery policy upon a government which embraces slaveholding and non-slaveholding States; and before he enthrones his ideal
theories he must subvert the government and banish
the Constitution of the United States. All that the
South asks is, that the Constitution be upheld. All
that she asks is, a full participation in the benefits of a
common government, a full recognition of her rights,
and a clear vindication of her honor. Does anybody
believe that the Federal Government could have been
constructed if it had been understood that the powers
were to be directed against slavery in the States? The
Constitution provides for the representation of slaves as
an elementary part of the machinery of the government.
How then can it be asserted that this is an anti-slavery
government in its nature, and that it was put on the
wrong tract forty years since by admitting a slaveholding
State into the Union? If the government could not
have been constructed with an understanding that its

policy was to be directed against slavery, is it not a flagrant breach of good faith to seize the departments of that government, and turn them against it?"

Henry Ward Beecher, in 1861, said: "I wish our fathers had stood out against what is called the compromises of the Constitution. But our fathers signed the bond, and we accepted it. Can we afford to break it for even so magnificent a result as the emancipation of the slave? Shall we rend the crystal instrument— the joy of the world and our pride? It is very easy to say, 'Now it is a state of war, let us declare emancipation.' The war has not driven us out of our institutions. We are not ourselves in a state of rebellion. We cannot expect by destroying the Constitution to put down the rebellion. If any one asks me whether a law or a constitution is superior to original principles of morality and justice, I say, no; but plighted faith is itself in the nature of a sacred, moral principle. Our faith is given and must be kept. When we cannot abide by our promise, then, in methods expressly provided, we must withdraw the pledge and the agreements of the Constitution, and start apart as two separate people. We, who boast of our Constitution, must not violate it ourselves, in putting down those who violate it."

According to the moral philosophy then of this popular divine, whose opinions with many are equal to sacred law, the government has actually violated the Constitution, and broken the bond signed by our fathers. "Plighted faith is itself in the nature of a sacred moral principle. Our faith is given and must be kept." But Abraham Lincoln and his lawmakers have broken their plighted faith, and are therefore as morally guilty as

the South of rebellion against the Constitution of our
fathers. " We are not ourselves in a state of rebellion,"
said Mr. Beecher in 1861, but in 1864 we are, for we
have done the very acts which constitute rebellion, and
by force of arms are subverting the government our
fathers founded.

The price of the Union which our fathers founded
was the return of a negro now and then to his master.
The price of the Union which the Republicans have
founded is the enslavement of every able-bodied man
between the ages of eighteen and forty-five to the
United States Government. Washington said the black
slaves owed service to their masters—now, white slaves
owe service to the government. The shackles fall from
the black man only to be transferred to the white man.

Washington said: "I behold in the characters selected
to adopt the measures of government the surest pledges
that the foundations of our national policy will be laid
in the immutable principles of private morality ;" and
he adds, that " the preservation of the sacred fire of liberty, and the destiny of the republican model of government, are staked on the experiment intrusted to the
hands of the American people."

The Constitution was "the cement of the Union" by
which all the States were held together, to which they
all assented, and by which all were bound. Washington believed the Constitution to be founded in justice,
order and right; that every step by which the United
States had advanced to the character of an independent
nation had been distinguished by some token of providential agency. In his Farewell Address, in 1796, he
still prayed that Heaven would continue to the people of
the United States the choicest tokens of its beneficence;

that their union and brotherly love might be perpetual; that the free Constitution, which was the work of their hands, might be sacredly maintained; that it was of infinite moment that they should properly estimate the immense value of their National Union; that they should speak of it as of the palladium of their political safety and prosperity, watching for its preservation with jealous anxiety; discountenancing whatever may suggest a suspicion that it can in any event be abandoned, and indignantly frowning upon the first dawning of every attempt to enfeeble the sacred ties which now link together the various parts.—*George Washington.*

When Washington retired from the public supervition of the government he was the foremost in establishing, an illustrious patriot and signer of the Declaration of Independence was placed by the people in the Presidential chair as the worthy successor of the Father of his Country, whom he eulogizes, in his first address to the people, as the man whose great actions had conducted the people of America to independence and peace; to increasing wealth and unexampled prosperity; who merited the highest gratitude of his people, and had secured immortal glory with posterity.

He says: "With this great example before me, pledged to support the Constitution of the United States, I entertain no doubt of its continuance, and my mind is prepared, without hesitation, to lay myself under the most solemn obligations to support it to the utmost of my power. And may that Being who is supreme over all, the Patron of order, the Fountain of justice, and the Protector, in all ages of the world, of virtuous liberty, continue his blessing upon the nation and its government, and give it all possible success and

duration consistent with the ends of his providence."—
John Adams.

Four years more, and the government is placed in
the hands of another signer of the Declaration of Independence, and the immortal author of that immortal
production. He says upon the great occasion:

"A rising nation, spread over a wide and fruitful
land; traversing all the seas with the rich productions
of their industry; advancing rapidly to destinies beyond
the reach of mortal eye—when I contemplate these
transcendent objects, and see the honor, the happiness,
and the hopes of my beloved country, committed to the
issue and the auspices of this day, I shrink from the
contemplation, and humble myself before the magnitude
of the undertaking.

"Possessing a chosen country, with room enough for
our descendants to the hundredth and thousandth generation, acknowledging and adoring an overruling Providence—with all these blessings, what more is necessary
to make us a happy and prosperous people? The wisdom of our sages and the blood of our heroes have been
devoted to the attainment of these blessings—freedom
of religion, freedom of the press, and freedom of the
person under the protection of the habeas corpus, and
trial by jury, the supremacy of the civil over the military authority. These principles form the bright con-
stellation which has gone before us. They should be
the creed of our political faith, the touchstone to try the
services of those we trust; and should we wander from
them in moments of error or alarm, let us hasten to
retrace our steps, and to regain the road which leads to
peace, liberty, and safety.

"I shall need the favor of that Being who led our
4

fathers, as Israel of old, from their native land, and
planted them in a country flowing with all the necessaries of life, who has covered our infancy with his
providence and our riper years with his wisdom and
power; and I ask you to join in supplications with me,
that he will so enlighten the minds of your servants,
guide their counsels and prosper their measures, that
whatsoever they do shall result in your good, and shall
secure to you the peace, friendship, and approbation of
all nations."—*Thomas Jefferson.*

Another "signer" takes his seat and holds the reins
of government, and he bestows upon his immediate
predecessor the tribute of his sympathy, which he en-
joyed in the benedictions of a beloved country, grate-
fully bestowed for exalted talents, zealously devoted,
through a long career, to the advancement of the highest
interests and happiness of his country. "My confidence
will be placed in the virtue of my fellow-citizens, next
to that of the guardianship of that Almighty Being
whose power regulates the destiny of nations, whose
blessings have been so conspicuously dispensed to this
rising republic, and to whom we are bound to address
our devout gratitude for the past, and our fervent supplications and hopes for the future."—*James Madison.*

Twenty-eight years of unparalleled happiness and
prosperity, brought about by the wisdom and virtue of
the rulers of America, induced the people to select their
fifth President from the same State where three of their
former ones were born—and a Virginian ruled the nation
for eight years longer. Soon after his inauguration he
visited the Northern States, and was met throughout his
tour by civic processions, military escorts, and enthusi-
astic crowds. The Society of the Cincinnati, at New

York, presented him with an address, and he referred, in the reply which he made, to the times of Washington, and his own former connection, in the battle-field, with many of the persons whom he saw before him. In reply to an address of the people of Maine, he said: "The further I advance in my progress in the country, the more I perceive that we are all Americans; that we compose but one family; that our republican institutions will be supported and perpetuated by the united zeal and patriotism of all. Nothing could give me greater satisfaction than to behold a perfect union among ourselves—a union which is necessary to restore to social intercourse its former charms (before the war with England in 1812), and to render our happiness as a nation unmixed and complete. To promote this desirable result requires no compromise of principle, and I promise to give it my continued attention and my best endeavors." This assurance was honestly made and honestly carried out. When he retired from the Presidency in 1825, he left the country in a high state of prosperity, and carried with him the respect and regard of the nation. Jefferson said: "If the soul of James Monroe was turned inside out, not a spot would be found on it."

The very year which wafted the pure soul of James Monroe to the home of the purified in heaven, there was wafted over this nation the death-cry of the Union. The proffer of this pure, of this beloved patriot slaveholder, that the whole American people should compose but one family, that there should be a perfect union among ourselves, and that our happiness as a nation might be complete, was insolently rejected by the rebel leaders against the Union, whose cry went forth upon the breeze: "No Union with slaveholders."

Thirty-four years from the time that Washington addressed his farewell to the American people, praying that the Constitution, which was the work of their hands, might be sacredly maintained, there arose a demon from the bottomless pit, bearing in his hands a banner with an inscription written in blood-red characters: "The Constitution of the United States is a Covenant with Death and an Agreement with Hell;" and to that inscription was signed the name of Wm. Lloyd Garrison.

Washington told his people that it was of infinite moment that they should properly estimate the immense value of their national Union, and this rebel demon responded: "The Union is a curse. If such a process were necessary to restore liberty to the captive, I would tread the Union and the Constitution which you formed under my feet as soon as I would a viper that stung me." "I know there is much declamation about the sacredness of the compact which you and your co-partners formed between the free and the slave States, upon the adoption of the Constitution. I recognize the compact with feelings of shame and indignation, and it will be held in everlasting infamy by the friends of justice and humanity throughout the world. You had no power to bind yourselves and your posterity for one hour by such an unholy alliance. It was not valid then, it is not valid now. Such a compact was in the nature of things null and void from the beginning."

Washington said to his children: "I pray that your union and brotherly affection may be perpetual. You have fought and triumphed together; the independence and liberty you possess are the work of joint counsels, of joint efforts, of common dangers, sufferings and successes."

And Garrison replied: "We have no love for the white people of the South. We love the negroes—they are our brothers. Let the Union be accursed. God demands a ballot-box in which the slaveholders shall never cast a ballot." "They are men-stealers, robbers, and kidnappers, and, unless they repent, will have their part in the lake which burneth with fire and brimstone."

William Lloyd Garrison tells his own story, in 1861, and we are to listen. He says: "I began this work in an uncompromising spirit. The slaveholder in vain pleaded that he held his slaves by a divine right, under both dispensations, under Moses and by the sanction of Jesus Christ. In vain he told me that his right to hold his slaves consisted in this, that he had bought them fairly, and that they were his property. In vain he pleaded that to emancipate his slaves would only be to make their condition wretched and miserable. To all his pleas I simply gave the lie, and declared that there could be no such thing as property in man—that it is the right of every slave to be instantly freed, and that therefore there could be no compromise whatever. I did not say, simply, that slavery, as a system, is wrong, but that the act of holding human beings as slaves was a sin against God—a crime of the deepest dye." (If so, then what criminals were Washington, Madison, Jefferson, Monroe, and Clay, the patriots who founded this best government on earth!)

"If I had only said that slavery was an evil to be deplored, and some time or other, in the distant future, to be abolished, he would have responded in the affirmative, and we should have had no controversy; but it was the doctrine of instant, unconditional emancipation, that made him see, as it were, the handwriting on the wall.

At last I was brought to see the government of the country stood directly in the way of the slave's emancipation. What could I do? If, in looking into the Constitution of the country, I saw there compromises and guarantees whereby the slaveholders were enabled to possess themselves of their slave property securely, and to extend and enlarge their slave system: what else could I do than to cry out against it, and pronounce such an instrument a covenant with death and an agreement with hell? And so the slave was put into one scale, and the Government, the Constitution, and the Union into the other. They kicked the beam and he outweighed them all."

Garrison says he began the work of emancipating the slave by overthrowing the Government, the Constitution, and the Union. Mark, now, his progress from 1833, and see that Abraham Lincoln is his agent, and is carrying out his plan. It is said that the South commenced to prepare for war thirty years ago. That evinced their wisdom and foresight, for against William Lloyd Garrison's abolition army they must fight or be destroyed. If Garrison should succeed in overthrowing the government which they had helped to form, their own destruction followed, of course.

On the second day of December, 1835, George Wolf, Governor of Pennsylvania, sent forth his annual message, and contained therein was the following account of the progress which Garrison and his followers were making. He says:

"For some time past, certain individuals, under the cognomen of abolitionists, have been laboring most assiduously to impress upon the public mind the necessity of the immediate emancipation of the slaves in the

South. Inhabiting a State which was the first to abolish slavery, we cannot be affected by the existing excitement otherwise than as members of the great American confederacy, and as forming a link in the great chain which binds it together. As such we are deeply interested in the peace, the unity, and integrity of the whole. This most delicate, and I may say unfortunate, subject formed a part of the policy of the South, before and at the time of our great political association. The sages of the Revolution, to whom the arrangement and detail of the political compact were entrusted, were aware of its existence in the fullest extent. They were no strangers to the servile condition of the slave, nor to the burdens inflicted on the master. They were well convinced that there existed rights and interests which could not be abrogated or abridged without preventing forever the establishment of that union which they were anxious to cement. These rights were admitted, these interests conceded before the great bond of union which it was their purpose to form and perpetuate could be harmonized and reconciled. These rights remain as sacred now as they were then, and we are solemnly bound by the obligations to justice, humanity, and good faith, to abstain from interfering, in any manner, with them.

"The present crusade against slavery is the offspring of fanaticism of the most dangerous and alarming character; which, if not speedily checked, may kindle a fire which it may require the best blood in the country to quench, and engender feelings which may prove fatal to the Union. Let public opinion check the further progress of this misdirected enthusiasm."—*George Wolf, Harrisburg*, Dec. 2, 1835.

The best blood of the country has failed yet to quench
the fire of rebellion which these wicked abolitionists
kindled.   Who loved the Union then—the Governor of
Pennsylvania and his friends who were Democrats, or
the abolitionists who now denounce them?   This war
would never have been but for these "fanatics," and is
the offspring of their fanaticism.   All those who would
preserve the Union by abstaining from all interference
with the slaves of the South—who wished to keep inviolate the compact made by the fathers of the republic—
were denounced as pro-slavery and wicked hypocrites.

In the same month, General Jackson, President of the
United States, addressed the people as follows: "I
must invite your attention to the painful excitement
produced in the South by the attempts to circulate
through the mails inflammatory appeals addressed to the
passions of the slaves.   There is doubtless no respectable
portion of our own countrymen, who can be so far
misled as to feel any other sentiment than that of
indignant regret at conduct so destructive of the harmony
and peace of our country—so repugnant to the principles
of our national compact, and to the dictates of humanity
and religion.   Our happiness and prosperity depend
upon peace within our borders, and peace depends upon
the maintenance, in good faith, of those compromises of
the Constitution upon which the Union is founded.

"It is fortunate for the country that the good sense,
the generous feeling, and the deep-rooted attachment of
the people of the non-slaveholding States to the Union,
and to their fellow-citizens of the same blood in the
South, have given so strong and impressive a tone to the
sentiments entertained against the proceedings of the
misguided persons who have engaged in these unconsti-

tutional and wicked attempts, and especially against the
emissaries from foreign parts (George Thompson and
others) who have dared to interfere in this matter, as
to authorize the hope that those attempts of these
fanatics will no longer be persisted in. But if these
expressions of the public will shall not be sufficient to
effect so desirable a result, not a doubt can be entertained that the North, so far from countenancing the
slightest interference with the constitutional rights of
the South, will be prompt to exercise its authority in
suppressing, so far as in it lies, *whatever is calculated to
produce this evil.*"—*Andrew Jackson,* Dec. 9, 1835.

There is the name of the great warrior and statesman
set to a document condemning William Lloyd Garrison,
George Thompson, and their great army enlisted under
their banner, as fanatics—who were engaged in wicked
and unconstitutional proceedings, destructive of the
harmony and peace of our country, repugnant to the
principles of our national compact, as well as to the
dictates of humanity and religion; and hoping that the
North will suppress, by an exercise of its authority,
whatever is calculated to destroy the peace, which
" depends upon the maintenance, in good faith, of those
compromises of the Constitution on which the Union is
founded." Had the advice of that old hero been taken
thus early, these abolitionists would not now be deplor-
ing that he is not alive to put down this rebellion which
their fanaticism kindled. All their publications would
have been suppressed, as they now suppress the Democratic papers, which tried for thirty years to save the
Union from destruction by these very abolitionists.

On the 9th of January, 1836, James Buchanan made
the following remarks in the Senate of the United

States: "A number of fanatics, led on by foreign incendiaries, have been scattering 'firebrands, arrows, and
death throughout the Southern States.' Self-preserva-
tion is the first law of nature. The people of the South
must counteract the efforts of the abolitionists. The
slaves must be kept in closer bondage to prevent their
rising. The property of the master in his slave existed
in full force before the Federal Constitution was adopted.
These States, by the adoption of the Constitution, never
yielded to the general government any right to interfere
with their slaves. The Constitution has, in the clearest
terms, recognized the right of property in the slaves.
Do not the abolitionists perceive, that the spirit roused
at the South must protract to an indefinite period the
emancipation of the slave? The necessary effect of
their efforts is to render desperate those to whom the
power of emancipation belongs."

Twenty-five years passed away, and the South was in
such a state of desperation that James Buchanan, though
President of the United States, had not power to control
it; and the abolitionists called him a traitor because he
could not quench those fierce flames these fanatics had
kindled by their firebrands, scattered for so long a period
throughout the Southern States. In June, 1833, the
editor of the Richmond Whig said:

"Garrison, himself, is not more a friend of emancipation than we, but we happen to live in the South, and
to know, beyond the possibility of being mistaken, that,
if ever achieved, it must be done by the voluntary action
of the slaveholder, and that *every* external attempt to
accelerate it—no matter from what quarter—renders
more desperate the now wellnigh desperate chance of
success by colonization. This is as true as there is a

heaven above, and it ought at once to seal the lips of the whole tribe of fanatics."

In April, 1836, Gerrit Smith said: "It is not to be disguised, sir, that war has broken out between the South and the North, not easily to be terminated. Political men, for their own purposes, are industriously striving to restore peace. The sword now drawn will not be sheathed till victory—entire victory—is ours or theirs. Whom shall we muster on our side in this great battle between liberty and slavery?"

This great infidel, who said that if he were elected President by the abolitionists, his first effort would be made for the overthrow of the Christian religion, was thus early enlisted under the banner of Garrison, and mustering men into the abolition crusade against the South. But there was one man who did not join them then, and of course would not fight for them now, were the old hero yet among the living. Hear his farewell warning to the people of the United States against this abolition army:

"Fellow-citizens," says General Jackson, again, in 1839: "Being about to retire finally from public life, if I use the occasion to offer you the counsels of age and experience, you will, I trust, receive them with the same indulgent kindness you have so often extended to me; and will, at least, see in them an earnest desire to perpetuate in this favored land the blessings of liberty and equal law. We have now lived almost fifty years under the Constitution framed by the sages and patriots of the Revolution. It is no longer a doubtful experiment. And at the end of nearly half a century we find that it has preserved unimpaired the liberties of the people, secured the rights of property, and that our country has improved, and is flourishing beyond any former example in the history of nations. (Although ruled for forty years by slaveholders, and the Constitution a covenant with death, and an agreement with hell.)

" It is no longer a question whether this great country can remain happily united, and flourish under our present form of government. Experience, the unerring test of all human undertakings, has shown the wisdom and foresight of those who formed it, and has proved that in the union of these States there is a sure foundation for the brightest hopes of freedom, and for the happiness of the people. At every hazard, and by every sacrifice, this Union must be preserved. The necessity of watching with jealous anxiety for the preservation of the Union was earnestly pressed upon his fellow-citizens by the Father of his Country, in his farewell address, and he there told us there would always be reason to distrust the patriotism of those who, in any quarter, may endeavor to weaken its bonds. When we look upon the scenes that are passing around us, and dwell upon the pages of his parting address, his paternal counsels would seem to be not merely the offspring of wisdom and foresight, but the voice of prophecy, foretelling events, and warning us of the evil to come. Forty years have passed since this imperishable document was given to his countrymen. The Federal Constitution was then regarded by him as an experiment, and he so speaks of it in his address; but an experiment upon the success of which the best hopes of his country depended. The trial has been made. It has succeeded beyond the proudest hopes of those who framed it. Every quarter of this wide nation has felt its blessings, and shared in the prosperity produced by its adoption. But amid the general prosperity, the dangers of which he warned us are becoming every day more evident, and the signs of evil are sufficiently apparent to awaken the deepest anxiety in the bosom of the patriot. We behold systematic attempts to sow the seeds of discord between different parts of the United States, and to place party divisions directly upon geographical distinctions, to excite the *South* against the *North*, and the North against the South, and to force into the controversy the most delicate and exciting topics—topics which it is impossible that a large portion of the Union can ever speak of without strong emotion. Appeals, too, are constantly made to sectional interests, in order to influence the election of the Chief Magistrate, as if it were desired that he should favor a particular quarter of the country, instead of fulfilling his station with impartial justice to all: and the possible dissolution of the Union has at length become an ordinary and familiar subject of discussion. Has the warning voice of Washington been forgotten, or have designs already been formed to sever the Union?

Now, where do we find the motto, "The Union must be preserved," so often quoted now by abolitionists, except in the very warning given in his Farewell Address, against these very abolitionists, who were talking about the possible dissolution of this Union, but the fanatics enlisted under the banner of Wm. Lloyd Garrison? It has been said that General Jackson wrote a letter, in which he declared that the next pretext South Carolina would make for dissolving the Union would be the slavery question, and that letter was dated 1833. But here, four years later, he was warning the country

against disunionists North; and he commenced the
warning two years before—not against Southern traitors, but against Northern ones.   To whom is he
addressing himself, when he says—" What have you to
gain by division and dissension?   Delude not yourself
that a breach once made may be afterwards repaired.
If the Union is once severed, the line of separation will
grow wider and wider, and the controversies which are
now debated and settled in the halls of legislation, will
then be tried in fields of battle, and determined by the
sword.   It is impossible to look on the consequences
that would inevitably follow the destruction of this
government, and not feel indignant when we hear cold
calculations about the value of the Union, and have so
constantly before us a line of conduct so well calculated
to weaken its ties."

Behold the indignation manifested here by that great
statesman against the conduct of the abolitionists, who
were thereby weakening the ties of the Union!   " But
the Constitution cannot be maintained, nor the Union
preserved in opposition to public feeling, by the mere
exertion of the coercive power of the government.   The
foundations must be laid in the affections of the people,
in the security it gives to life, liberty, character and
property, in every quarter of the country; and in
the fraternal attachment which the citizens of the
several States bear to one another, as members of one
political family, mutually contributing to promote the
happiness of each other.   Hence, the citizens of every
State should studiously avoid every thing calculated to
wound the sensibilities, or offend the just pride of the
people of other States; and they should frown upon any
proceedings within their borders likely to disturb the

tranquillity of their political brethren in other portions of the Union.   In a country so extensive as the United States, the internal regulations of the several States must frequently differ from each other, and this difference is unavoidably increased by the varying principles upon which the American colonies were originally planted, principles which have taken deep root in their social relations before the Revolution, and, therefore, of necessity influencing their policy since they became free and independent States.   But each State has the unquestionable right to regulate its own internal concerns according to its own pleasure, and while it does not interfere with the rights of the people of other States, or the rights of the Union, every State must be the sole judge of the measures proper to secure the safety of its citizens, and promote their happiness; and all efforts on the part of the people of other States to cast odium upon their institutions, and all measures calculated to disturb their rights of property, or to put in jeopardy their peace and internal tranquillity, are in direct opposition to the spirit in which the Union was formed, and must endanger its safety.   Rest assured that the men found busy in this work of discord are not worthy of your confidence, and deserve your strongest reprobation."—*Andrew Jackson.*

Who were those men declared by General Jackson deserving the strongest reprobation of the American people? They were Wm. Lloyd Garrison, Wendell Phillips, Theodore Parker, George P. Cheever, Gerrit Smith, and hosts of lesser workers of discord following after them.

In these days it is considered a great crime to be disloyal to the government of the United States, and everybody is required to acquiesce in every measure Abraham Lincoln considers necessary to save the Union. Was not General Jackson's authority equal to that of Mr. Lincoln? Is he not considered as wise a statesman to-day, even wiser, and the absence of his counsels and wisdom in this great emergency universally deplored? But how were his counsels treated, when standing up for the last time, in the exact place where Mr. Lincoln is now pretending to be engaged in saving the Union from destruction, he appealed to the citizens of America to frown upon any proceedings likely to weaken the ties of the Union, or disturb the rights of the property, or put in jeopardy the peace of the people in the South. The abolitionists all over the North replied to his appeals and responded to his counsels in the following decided resolve:

"'That it is the duty of every person who makes any pretensions to republicanism, or the common feelings of humanity, to exercise all their influence in all their capacities, to effect the abolition of all the slave laws in our country, and the immediate and unconditional emancipation of all the slaves;" and this after General Jackson had told them that each State had a right to regulate its own internal concerns according to its own pleasure. He told them that the foundations of the Union must be preserved by the fraternal attachment which the citizens of the several States should bear to one another, as members of one political family, mutually contributing to promote the happiness of each other. And they answered him by resolving, "That it is the duty of every citizen who has the right to vote, to exercise that right in favor of no candidate for the offices of President, Governor, Federal or State Legislature or any other station that gives a political power over slavery, except he be opposed to that system in abstract feeling and outward action;" and, again, that they would vote for no slaveholder for office, or for any person that would vote for a slaveholder. That is the loyalty displayed towards the government of the United States when a Democratic President ruled over the people instead of an abolitionist.

In the Life of John Adams, one of the founders of the government, it declares that "a settled plan to deprive the people of all the benefits and ends of the contract, to subvert the fundamentals of the Constitution, to deprive them of all share in making and executing the laws, will justify a revolution."

The progress the abolitionists were making towards the dissolution of the Union in eight years can be estimated by the speech of Hon. Henry Clay, in the United States Senate, in 1839. He says:

"The abolitionists are resolved to persevere in the pursuit of their object at all hazards; their purpose is to manumit forthwith, and without compensation, and without moral preparation three millions of negro slaves, under jurisdictions altogether separate from those under which they live. I have said that the abolition of slavery in the District of Columbia and the exclusion of new States, were only means towards the attainment of their end. Unfortunately, they are not the only means. Another and a much more lamentable one is, that of arraying one portion against another portion of the Union. With that view, in all their leading prints the alleged horrors of slavery are depicted in the most glowing and exaggerated colors, to excite the imaginations and stimulate the rage of the people in the free

5

States against the people in the slave States. The slaveholder is held up and represented as the most atrocious of human beings. Advertisements of slaves to be sold are carefully collected and blazoned forth, to infuse a spirit of detestation and hatred against one entire section of the Union.

" I would seriously invite every considerate man in the country solemnly to pause and reflect, not merely on our existing posture, but upon that dreadful precipice down which they would hurry us. To the agency of their powers of persuasion they now propose to substitute the powers of the ballot-box, and the inevitable tendency of their proceedings is, if these should be found insufficient, to invoke, finally, the more potent powers of the bayonet.

" The first impediment in the way of the abolitionists of the emancipation of the slaves, is the utter and absolute want of all power in the General Government to effect their purpose. The Constitution of the United States creates a limited government, comprising comparatively few powers, and leaving the residuary mass of political power in the possession of the several States. It is well known that the subject of slavery interposed one of the greatest difficulties in the formation of the Constitution. It was happily compromised and adjusted in a spirit of harmony and patriotism. According to that compromise, no power whatever was granted to the General Government in respect to domestic slavery but that which relates to taxation and representation, and the power to restore fugitive slaves to their owners. All other power in regard to the institution of slavery was retained exclusively by the States, to be exercised by them according to their own peculiar interest. The

Constitution of the United States never could have been formed upon the principle of investing the General Government with authority to abolish the institution at its pleasure. It never can be continued for a single day if the exercise of such a power be assumed or usurped."

Henry Clay was considered by all the people of these United States, and, during the latter part of his life, by the Republicans in particular, to be the wisest statesman in America. There is his authority, then, to prove that Abraham Lincoln has destroyed the Constitution of our country. He has assumed the power and usurped authority to abolish slavery in all the States he pleases, and if the people continue him as President four years longer, there is not a doubt that he will usurp the authority and assume the power to trample all law under his feet.

Henry Clay asks: "Why are the slave States wantonly and cruelly assailed? Why do the abolition presses teem with publications tending to excite hatred and animosity on the part of the inhabitants of the free States against those of the slave States? I know that there is a visionary dogma which holds that negro slaves cannot be the subjects of property. Under all the forms of government which have existed upon this continent for two hundred years they have been solemnly recognized as property. They were treated as property in the very British example which is appealed to as worthy of imitation. Although the West India planters had no voice in Parliament, an irresistible sense of justice extorted from that legislature the grant of twenty millions of pounds sterling to the colonists for their loss of property.

" Sir, I am not in the habit of speaking lightly of the possibility of dissolving this happy Union; but abolition should no longer be regarded as an imaginary danger. The abolitionists, let me suppose, succeed in their present aim of uniting the people of the free States as one man against the people of the slave States. Union on one side will beget union on the other; and this process of reciprocal consolidation will be attended with all the implacable animosities which ever degraded or deformed human nature. The collision of opinion will be quickly followed by the clash of arms. I will not attempt to describe scenes which now happily lie concealed from our view. Abolitionists themselves would shrink back in dismay and horror at the contemplation of desolated fields, conflagrated cities, murdered inhabitants, and the overthrow of the fairest fabric of human government that ever rose to animate the hopes of civilized man. Nor should these abolitionists flatter themselves that, if they can succeed in their object of uniting the people of the North against the people of the South, they will enter the contest with a numerical superiority that must insure victory. All history and experience prove the hazard and uncertainty of war. And we are admonished by holy writ that ' the race is not to the swift, nor the battle to the strong." But if they were to conquer, whom would they conquer? A foreign foe? No, sir. It would be a conquest without laurels, without glory; a suicidal conquest; a conquest of brothers over brothers, achieved by one over another portion of the descendants of common ancestors, who, nobly pledging their lives, their fortunes, and their sacred honors, had fought and bled, side by side, in many a hard battle on land and ocean, and established our independence.

"Mr. President, the Searcher of all hearts knows that every pulsation of my heart beats high and strong in the cause of civil liberty. Wherever it is safe and practicable, I desire to see every portion of the human family in the enjoyment of it. But I prefer the liberty of my own race to that of any other race. The liberty of the descendants of Africa in the United States is incompatible with the liberty and safety of the European descendants. We did not originate, nor are we responsible for its necessity. Their liberty, if it were possible, could only be established by violating the incontestible powers of the States, and subverting the Union; and beneath the ruins of the Union would be buried, sooner or later, the liberty of both races."

Now, this accomplished scholar, this learned lawyer, this profound statesman, has told the people fairly what would be the result of forcible emancipation of the slaves in the South. Abraham Lincoln can only establish their freedom by "violating the incontestible powers of the States, and subverting the Union; and beneath the ruins of the Union" he is to reign supreme over both black and white—north and south, east and west. To avoid this dire result, Mr. Clay appealed to the abolitionists in this touching strain: "I beseech the abolitionists themselves to pause in their mad and fatal course. Let them select some object of humanity that does not threaten to deluge our country in blood. I call upon that small portion of the clergy which has lent itself to these wild and ruinous schemes, not to forget the holy nature of the divine mission of the Founder of our religion, and to profit by his peaceful examples. I entreat that portion of my countrywomen, who have given their countenance to abolition, to reflect that the

ink which they shed in subscribing with their fair hands
abolition petitions may prove but the prelude to the
shedding of the blood of their brethren.   I adjure all
the inhabitants of the free States to rebuke and discoun-
tenance measures which must inevitably lead to the most
calamitous consequences.   And let us all, as countrymen, as friends, and as brothers, cherish in unfading
memory the motto which bore our ancestors trium-
phantly through all the trials of the Revolution, and, if
adhered to, it will conduct their posterity through all
that may, in the dispensation of Providence, be reserved
for them."

Five years passed away, and the abolitionists had not
paused in their course to overthrow the government and
dissolve the Union.   Horace Greeley could denounce
their course, and say " that the tendencies of abolition
are toward a sweeping, radical revolution both in Church
and State.   The abolition policy is the exact antipodes
of that uniformly pursued by Clarkson and Wilberforce
and their fellow philanthropists in Great Britain.   We
have already noticed the formation of a new society in
the town of Skaneatelas.   This society is an offshoot of
the ultra anti-slavery spirit of the time ; and embodies
a protest against all civil government—all authority in
Church and State."   Their sentiments are thus set forth
in their publications :

" Rejecting the hoary doctrine of man's natural de-
pravity, we assert that human nature is pure, noble,
divine ; that human rights are equal the world over ;
that all sects and parties, civil and ecclesiastical, priests
and politicians, churches and governments, are mon-
strosities of ignorance and bigotry."

Mr. Greeley says : " That the No-Church movement

had its origin in abolition, we perceive as clearly as we do the causes of any great moral and social impulse. The career of the Vermont Telegraph, of Wm. Lloyd Garrison and his Liberator, the Herald of Freedom, the course of Gerrit Smith—all prove it."

Some abolitionists say, " No union with slaveholders ;" Gerrit Smith says, " Be ours the better motto, No slaveholder for civil office, and no person who thinks a slaveholder fit for one." Mr. Greeley says, " No person who thinks a slaveholder fit for office can be voted for by a liberty man. It is not enough that to cast a vote for Washington, Patrick Henry, Jefferson, or John Marshall, is to brand a man a traitor to freedom ; but to vote for *any man who would* vote for any of these is to be a traitor. The blacks must surely be overwhelmed with gratitude towards such champions of their rights."

Again he says: " The abolitionists say that Henry Clay is unfit to be the President because he is a slaveholder. Is this the way to preserve the Union ? If a noble and lofty statesman can be hunted down on such grounds as these, is not the Union, in essence, dissolved ? How shall we ask the South to support a Northern man for President, or *submit* to the rule of one, if the bare fact that a candidate is a Southern man is to exclude him from the honors of the republic ?"

Again : " In their State Conventions, the abolitionists soberly tell us that one clause in the Constitution is null and void (the rendition of a fugitive slave), because it seems in their view to recognize slavery, and yet would have us believe that an abolition President of their making would coolly stand up and swear, with solemn oath, that he believed that Constitution, and would maintain it. Men begin to inquire whether they would dare to put a candidate of the abolition party into the presidential chair. Would it not be an act so rash in its character and fearful in its results that we should hesitate to assume the responsibility? Shall my assumption that the government is morally wrong in one of its requisitions justify me in swearing to obey that government in order to obtain a coveted office, and then proceeding to disobey it? How can I take an oath to obey and preserve inviolate the Constitution of the United States, and yet purpose to disobey and violate one of the most important stipulations of that instrument, without which the Constitution would probably never have been framed and never adopted? What right have I to pick and choose which of its provisions I will obey and which disobey? How could James G. Birney take as President the oath to preserve the Constitution, all the while intending not to support, but to subvert certain parts of it? Would not this be perjury? And would Mr. Birney be any more culpable in taking the oath to support the Constitution, meaning all the while to violate a part of it, than would those who, by their votes, solemnly instructed and directed him to do so? In our judgment, all who vote to make Mr. Birney an abolition President vote to instruct him to commit perjury, and are themselves guilty (unwittingly) of subornation of perjury, just as much as if their purpose was consummated."

Now read the following, and see who voted to make Abraham Lincoln commit perjury. The Tribune, Dec. 3d, 1863, has the following:

"Thirty years ago to-day, a few men met in Philadelphia to form the American Anti-slavery Society. Eleven years after the formation of the society, kindred societies had been organized in every considerable town and village in the free States, whose members numbered scores of thousands. These associations had employed hundreds of agents, who had traversed the country, delivering addresses in all the principal centres of population. They had established newspapers in all the Northern States, and had circulated pamphlets and tracts by the million. Their principles had made a strong lodgment in the leading religious denominations of the country. The abolitionists aimed their blows right at the core of slavery, denouncing it as a sin, whose only appropriate remedy was immediate and unconditional emancipation, without expatriation. It requires no spirit of divination to perceive that the organization of the Anti-slavery Society in 1833, and the election of a Republican President in 1861, bear to each other the relation of remote cause and ultimate effect. The anti-slavery sentiment of the country consolidated its ranks, and Abraham Lincoln took the Presidential chair. Their great work hastens to completion."

Here we have the alarming fact revealed that the President of the United States, upon the very first of his election, was in the hands of an unprincipled set of men, who would not hesitate to direct him to violate his oath of office and commit perjury whenever their purposes required it. We have the fact revealed as clear as the light of day, that he is in the hands of men who inscribed upon their banners at that early day, "The Constitution of the United States is a covenant with death and an agreement with hell," that the government, the Union and the Constitution must all be overthrown in order to free the slaves. We have the solemn fact made known that the very men whom

General Jackson told us were not worthy of our confidence, and deserved our strongest reprobation for their wicked and unconstitutional attempts to produce insurrections in the South, and their endeavors to destroy the Union, are placed where they can carry out all their wicked schemes, under the sanction of laws of their own making. We have heard them shouting, "The Lord reigneth, let the earth rejoice! The covenant with death is annulled, the agreement with hell is broken. Let us not grieve over the Union of 1789." Were Henry Clay alive he could have heard William Lloyd Garrison say, "The slave States, with the exception of three or four, have all left the Union. I am glad of it. I did not believe in the old Union."

The government is in the hands of the enemies of all our patriot fathers, and of the Father of his Country in particular, whose counsels they have always despised. The following report is given of a meeting in Philadelphia in 1859:

"The meeting of the Anti-slavery Society was well attended, and many of the life-long defenders of the cause were present—William Lloyd Garrison among others. The report gave a full and lucid history of abolitionism in Pennsylvania from its origin. In 1789, the anti-slavery spirit was very animated. All classes were imbued with it, even to Tom Paine; yet from that period it became less energetic. Its decline is traced through many years of obscuration, and its revival is attributed to the establishment of the Boston Liberator, in 1831, and looks forward with prophetic confidence to the future."

Here is the link in the chain that reaches back to the days of Washington; and we have another startling fact brought to light, that tyrants and oppressors control the nation; for if the taking of one slave from Mr. Dalby was an act of tyranny and oppression, what is it to deprive the Southern people of four millions, less or more, without compensation? And it is against these tyrants and oppressors that the Southern people are fighting. They loved the Union up to the day of Abraham Lincoln's election, but they knew their fate, for it had been told them by the abolitionists themselves for thirty years. They asked security against their designs, by the Northern people. They failed to receive it, and resolved to protect themselves.

In the year 1835 Mr. Benton exposed the designs of the abolitionists in a speech made in the United States Senate, as follows:

"The abolitionists I cannot regard as any thing else but incendiaries and agitators, with diabolical objects in view, to be accomplished by wicked and deplorable means; for every attempt to work upon the passions of the slaves, and to excite them to murder their owners, was a wicked and diabolical attempt, and the work of a midnight incendiary. Pictures of slave degradation and misery, and of white man's luxury and cruelty, were attempts of this kind, for they were appeals to the vengeance of the slaves, and not to the intelligence and reason of those who legislated for them. Mr. Benton said he had many pictures of this kind, as well as many diabolical publications, sent to him on this subject during the last summer; the whole of which he had cast into the fire. And within a few days past, while abolition petitions were pouring into the Capitol, he had received one of the pictures, the design of which could be nothing but mischief of the blackest dye. The print was evidently from the abolition mint; and for what purpose could such a picture be intended, unless to inflame the passions of the slaves? And why engrave it, except to multiply copies for extensive circulation? But it was not pictures alone that operated upon the passions of the slaves, but speeches, publications, and the whole machinery of abolition societies, inspiring vague hopes, and stimulating insurrections. It was thus that the massacre of San Domingo was made. The society in Paris—Les Amis des Noirs—(friends of the blacks), with its affiliated societies throughout France, made that massacre. And who composed that society? In the beginning it comprised the extremes of virtue and vice—it contained the best and the basest of mankind: Lafayette and the Abbe Gregoire, those purest of philanthropists, and Marat and Anacharsis Cloots, those imps of hell in human shape. In the end, the good men, disgusted with their associates, retired from the scene, and the wicked ruled at pleasure. Declamations against slavery, pictures, publications in gazettes, petitions to the constituent assembly, were the mode of proceeding. The effect upon the French islands is known to the world."

An abolition writer in 1862, says: "The negroes did not revolt, did not rise in insurrection, did not murder, rob, and expel the whites from the Island of St. Domingo until 1801, seven years after their emancipation, when Bonaparte decreed their re-enslavement; and even then it was not till after the French had been guilty of the most horrible outrages against the negroes, that they retaliated in kind. Such is the true history of St. Domingo."

Now the truth is, that the abolitionists and republi-

cans who are now all as one, should have destroyed the
records of this nation, before they undertook to destroy
the government made by Washington, and the rest of
our illustrious forefathers—for while the Father of his
Country was still its Chief Executive, and sitting in the
same chair of state now occupied by Abraham Lincoln,
there then occurred that darkest of all dark tragedies,
known in history as the Massacre of St. Domingo.
Even Horace Greeley attempts to conceal its horrors, and
says: "Some nervous folks have been very much frightened by the raising of negro troops, and have sobbed
St. Domingo most piteously, under the impression that
a great many people were killed on that island, although
the mourners usually show a miraculous ignorance as to
who were killed, why they were killed, and who killed
them."

Well, Mr. Greeley, the mourners over that awful
catastrophe in the dark days of its occurrence were
General George Washington, the Father of this once
happy country, and his bosom friend, who loved him so
well when living that he wrote his memoirs after his
death, in which he says that "he was guided by an
unvarying sense of moral right, and by a purity of
virtue, which was not only untainted, but unsuspected."
In his Life of Washington, Chief Justice Marshall relates
the causes of the massacre of St. Domingo; he tells us
"who were killed, why they were killed, and who killed
them." And first he answers why they were killed;
and he says that these massacres were brought about by
the teachings of just such abolitionists as these in
America.

He says of the insurrection of the blacks in St.
Domingo: "Early and bitter fruit of that malignant

philosophy which, disregarding the actual state of the world, and estimating at nothing the miseries of a vast portion of the human race, can coolly and deliberately pursue, through oceans of blood, abstract systems, for the attainment of some fancied good, were gathered in the French West Indies. Instead of proceeding in the correction of any abuses which might exist by those slow and cautious steps which gradually introduce reform without ruin, the revolutionists of France formed the mad and wicked project of spreading their doctrines of equality among persons between whom distinctions and prejudices exist to be subdued only by the grave. The rage excited by the pursuit of this visionary and baneful theory burst forth on the 31st day of August, 1791, with a fury alike destructive and general.

"In one night, a preconcerted insurrection of the blacks took place throughout the colony, and the white inhabitants of the country, sleeping in their beds, were involved in one indiscriminate massacre, from which neither age nor sex could afford an exception. Only a few females, reserved for a fate more cruel than death, were spared, and not many were fortunate enough to escape into the fortified cities. The negroes then assembled in vast numbers, and a bloody war commenced between them and the whites. The whole French part of the island was in imminent danger of being totally lost to the mother country. The minister of his Most Christian Majesty applied to the President of the United States, General Washington, for a sum of money which would enable him to preserve this valuable colony, to be deducted out of the debt due to his sovereign, and the request was granted.

General Washington to M. de Ternant, minister from France:

"MOUNT VERNON, *September*, 1791.

"SIR :—I have not delayed a moment since the receipt of your letter, in dispatching orders to the Secretary of the Treasury to furnish the money, and to the Secretary of War to deliver the arms and ammunition, which you have applied to me for; and am happy in the opportunity of testifying how well disposed the United States are to render every aid in their power to our friends and allies, the French, to quell the alarming insurrection of the negroes in Hispaniola, and of the ready disposition of the executive authority to effect it.

"GEORGE WASHINGTON."

Now behold the awful contrast: Washington arming the whites against the blacks, to quell a servile insurrection; Abraham Lincoln arming the blacks against the whites, and trying to produce just such a scene of horror in the United States as occurred in St. Domingo. Washington was trying to save the white people from the baleful effects of the malignant philosophy taught by the French infidels. Abraham Lincoln carries out the wicked projects of the same class of infidels in America, whom Thomas Benton designated as incendiaries with diabolical objects in view, who had formed an abolition society in America, precisely like that in France to which belonged those imps of hell in human shape, Marat and Cloots; and history proves the principles of infidels in France identical with the abolition reformers in America. Anacharsis Cloots declared himself the "personal enemy of Jesus Christ," the spokesman of the human race, which he was determined to unite in one common brotherhood; and Theodore Parker says: "I do not take Jesus Christ for my master, I do not take the Bible for my master, I do not believe in the miraculous inspiration of the Old or New Testament."

The infidels of France celebrated the festival of Reason in the ancient cathedral of Notre Dame, instead of Divine service. They dethroned the Almighty, and set up for worship the Goddess of Reason. Gerrit Smith says: "May I make my Bible my standard? Certainly not until my reason has passed upon it. The Bible is the servant, and not the master of human reason. To honor my reason is at all times my religious duty." "The South is full of the common religion, and hence the impossibility of peacefully dislodging her slavery. It is true that the religion of France was not essentially different from that of our own country; but so slender was its hold on the public mind, that it could not prevent the reason of France from abolishing slavery. The abolition of French slavery is largely owing to French infidelity. Had that nation been more religious and less rational, her slavery would have continued to this day."

This was said by Gerrit Smith several years ago, and is an acknowledgment that the infidels of America were seeking the "dislodgment of slavery" in our country through the same means that were used by those in France. And if there was nothing else wanting to show that this war is a war of infidelity, and not a Christian war, these facts prove it. The beloved friend of Washington says: "The revolutionists of France formed the mad and wicked project of spreading their doctrines of equality among persons between whom distinctions and prejudices existed, to be subdued only by the grave."

As Judge Marshall was the intimate companion of Washington, he must have known his opinions; and these two officers, who fought for the independence of this nation, and understood the meaning of that phrase in the Declaration, "All men are created equal," here declare the inequality of the white and black race; declare that there existed between them distinctions and prejudices to be subdued only by the grave; that to spread the doctrines of equality among them was mad and wicked; that the philosophy which teaches such equality is a malignant philosophy; and that the theory is visionary and baneful.

And these are the very doctrines, this the very philosophy, which has been taught by the abolitionists of America for the last thirty years; which has been infused through all the American churches, until the doctrine that "all men are created equal" has been received as a religious dogma, and its belief made the test of Christian fellowship. And it has been taught, furthermore, that this bloody war, brought upon this nation by the promulgation of the false and malignant doctrines of the abolitionists, is a holy war, brought upon us by the Almighty, for the very purpose of carrying out the plans of men who scorn his revealed Word and trample the authority of Jesus Christ under their feet. We are told that it is to obey the commands of the Almighty that the negroes are armed against their masters, when the Bible says to "Let as many servants as are under the yoke (of slavery) count their masters worthy of all honor, that the name of God and his doctrine be not blasphemed." The abolitionists have taught the slaves that they have a natural right to kill their masters and all who stand between them and freedom, thus instigat-

6

ing the negroes for thirty years to rise against the white
people of the South. How could the people of the
South love the people of the North, who taught their
negroes that it was perfectly right to murder them at
any time and then rob them of such property as they
could bring away? Washington said it was an act of
oppression for a man to entice a slave from his master.
What name, then, can be given to the crime of teaching
the slaves, not only to leave their masters, but to take
their lives also, if need be, to gain their freedom? Had
the negroes followed the advice of the people of the
North, the South would long ere this have been deluged
in the blood of men, women, and children, and the lands
been left to waste.   It is not a new idea, advanced since
this war begun, to get the negroes armed to kill the
inhabitants of the South.   John Brown attempted the
same thing three years before Mr. Lincoln commenced
it, and all efforts have been made by the abolitionists
for that purpose it was possible to be made after the
South had the precaution to drive them from their soil
whenever they made their appearance.

Jefferson penned the declaration that "We hold
these truths to be self-evident that all men are created
equal, that they are endowed by their Creator with
certain unalienable rights—among which are life, liberty,
and the pursuit of happiness." The abolitionists declare
that these assertions of our forefathers to their rights of
liberty of which Great Britain was depriving them,
apply equally to the negro race now in slavery, and that
they have a natural right to rebel against the white
people, and raise a servile war, involving the slaughter
of the white race, and that such a war, on their part,
would be both righteous and just. And Jefferson's

words, that the Almighty has no attributes which could take part with the oppressor in such a war, are often quoted to prove he believed the negro slaves would be justified in rising against their masters. The insurrection in St. Domingo was a servile war—a war of races. Judge Marshall says the negroes assembled in vast numbers, and a bloody war commenced between them and the whites. Now what does Thomas Jefferson do in such a war? Which side does he take, that of the negroes or that of the white people? He says, " When the insurrection of the negroes in St. Domingo assumed a very threatening appearance, the Assembly sent a deputy here to ask assistance of military stores and provisions. He addressed himself to M. de Ternant, who (the President being in Virginia, as I was also) applied to the Secretaries of Treasury and War. They furnished one thousand stands of arms, and other military stores, and placed forty thousand dollars in the treasury subject to the order of the French Minister. Before the vessel arrived in St. Domingo, the Assembly, further urged by the appearance of danger, sent two deputies more with larger demands, viz., eight thousand bayonets and fusils, two thousand musquators, three thousand pistols, three thousand sabres, twenty-four thousand barrels of flour, four hundred livres worth of Indian meal, rice, peas, etc., for the starving inhabitants, and a large quantity of plank to repair the buildings destroyed. They applied to M. de Ternant, and then, with his consent, to me, he and I having previously had a conversation on the subject. Congress resolved that a regular account of the money expended by the government be kept, and the President be requested to obtain a credit therefor, in the accounts between the French republic and the United States."

Again he says, " In the first moment of the insurrection, which threatened the colony of St. Domingo, we stepped forward to their relief, with arms and money, taking freely upon ourselves the risk of an unauthorized aid when delay would have been denial; we received, according to our best abilities, the wretched fugitives from the catastrophe, who, escaping from the swords and flames of civil war, threw themselves on us, naked and houseless, without food or friends, money or other means—their faculties lost and absorbed in the depth of their distresses."

Behold the picture painted by the immortal Jefferson! Pity touched his heart, sympathy filled his soul for the distresses of those homeless, naked, famishing, and friendless people of his own race, escaping from that awful catastrophe! He received them according to his best abilities, and sent arms to kill the savage negroes who had slaughtered their friends in cold blood. But the abolitionists of America take the part of the negroes in that bloody tragedy, where two thousand white people were massacred without a chance for resistance. Mr. Smith, a member of Congress at the time of the appropriation for aid, said, " Such a scene of distress had never before been seen in America. Three thousand fugitives had been at once landed on our shores, without the least previous expectation of their arrival. Fifteen hundred of these people are quite helpless. All were women and children, except three old men."

· "And these calamities were brought upon these people," says Mr. Marshall, " by the malignant philosophy of the French revolutionists, who taught the equality of the white and the black race." Such are the calamities, such the scenes, such the distresses which the abolitionists of America had in store for the people of the South. Such is the tragedy they have endeavored for thirty years to re-enact, among the people who helped to compose this happy Union, who helped to frame the best government on earth, who were once called our sisters and brothers, whom Washington entreated us to cease from reproaching on account of their institutions which were fastened upon them by the mother country in the infancy of their colonies, and for which there was but one remedy, and that the expatriation of the negro race. Washington prayed that the people of America would consider themselves as one family, and live in peace and harmony together, and they would have continued so to live had not the abolitionists been determined to introduce the servants of Washington and our forefathers into this great family as their equals and their brothers, thus thwarting the plan of colonization begun by the South, to free their slaves and send them to Africa as fast as they could obtain the means for that purpose. Respecting the equality of mankind, Butler's Analogy of Religion has the following:

" It is perfectly idle to object to the fact, that a plan or decree is contemplated in revelation, and that God should confer benefits on some individuals which are withheld from others. Did any man in his senses ever dream that the race, in all respects, are on an equality? Has there ever been a time when one man was just as rich as another, or as much honored? To talk of the perfect equality of men is one of the most unmeaning of all affirmations respecting the world. God has made differences, is still making them, and will continue to do so. The framework of society is organized on such a principle, that men cannot be equal. Even if the scheme of modern infidelity should be successful, if all society should be broken up, what principle of perpetuity could be devised? Man might better attempt to make all trees alike, and all hills plains, than to attempt to level society and bring the race into entire equality. To the end of time it will be true that some are poor and some are rich; that some will be endowed with gigantic intellects, and enriched with ancient and modern learning, while others will pine in want, or walk the humble paths of obscurity. If God can confer one blessing on one individual, which he withholds from another, we ask why he may not be a sovereign also in the dispensation of other favors? Men will go on to make experiments in philosophy till scheme after scheme shall be abandoned; they will frame schemes, until they arrive at the scheme of the New Testament; they will devise modes of alleviating misery, until they fall on the very plan suggested two thousand years before them; and they will form and abandon codes of morals, until they shall come at last to the moral maxims of the New Testament, and the world shall arrive at the conclusion that the highest wisdom is to sit down like children at the feet of the Son of God, " convinced that he is the wisest man, as well as the profoundest philosopher, who yields himself up in meekness and simplicity of spirit to the teachings of the Saviour."

Here, Dr. Barnes, in his introduction to the work of Bishop Butler, speaks of the doctrine of human equality as that of the modern infidels; and all their schemes for alleviating the miseries of the human race will have to be " abandoned until the world shall arrive at the conclusion that the highest wisdom is to adopt the scheme of the New Testament."

Dr. Wayland, in his Elements of Moral Science, says : "If the New Testament had proclaimed the unlawfulness of slavery, and taught slaves to resist the oppression of their masters, it would instantly have arrayed the two parties in deadly hostility throughout the civilized world; its announcement would have been the signal for servile war; and the very name of the Christian religion would have been forgotten amidst the agitations of universal bloodshed."

Here we have the fact acknowledged, that Christ and his Apostles did not proclaim the unlawfulness of slavery, and teach slaves to resist the oppression of their masters. Therefore, the abolitionists have not followed the example of the Son of God, and cannot expect their conduct to be approved of him. It is a fact, also, that can be clearly proved, that there could have been a compromise of all our national troubles, even after the secession of a few of the Southern States, had not these abolitionists prevented it; and that they desired a civil war in order to "dislodge" slavery. After the war had been determined on, but before any great battle had occurred, Wm. Lloyd Garrison, and the other abolitionists, said : " If God shall choose to wash slavery out by a river of human blood, we shall exclaim, as did the Psalmist of old, ' Oh, give thanks unto the Lord, for he is good; for his mercy endureth forever! To Him that overthrew Pharaoh and his hosts in the Red Sea; for his mercy endureth forever.' "

Now, the washing out of slavery by human blood is not the way that Christ and his Apostles planned to wash it out; and as Christ is God, it may reasonably be inferred that the scheme of the abolitionists will entirely fail; and although they have succeeded in shedding rivers of human blood, slavery will not thereby be washed away. If Dr. Wayland's system of morality and ethics can be relied on, this government has committed a far greater crime in the sight of God by thus shedding their brother's blood than the crime of slaveholding. He says: " The individual has no right to authorize society to do any thing contrary to the law of God; that is, men connected in societies are under the same moral law as individuals. What is forbidden to the one is forbidden also to the other. Hence it would seem that all wars are contrary to the revealed will of God, and that society has no right to commit to government the power to declare war. To all arguments in favor of war, it would be a sufficient answer: that God has forbidden it; and no consequences can possibly be conceived to arise from keeping his law, so terrible as those which must arise from violating it. War is granted to be a most calamitous remedy for evils, and the most awful scourge that can be inflicted on the human race. It will be granted, then, that the resort to it, if not necessary, must be intensely wicked." And of civil war, he says:

" Civil war is, of all evils which men inflict on themselves, the most horrible. It dissolves not only social, but domestic ties; overturns all the security of property; throws back for ages all social improvement, and accustoms men to view without disgust, and even pleasure, all that is atrocious and revolting. Napoleon, accustomed as he was to bloodshed, turned away with horror from the contemplation of civil war. This, then, cannot be considered the way designed by our Creator for rectifying social abuses."

Now, to that class of the people of the Northern States who are not infidels, but believe in the Christian religion, Dr. Wayland teaches the following moral precepts:

" When a revelation is made to us by language, it is taken for granted, that whatever is our duty will be signified to us by a command ; and, hence, what is not commanded, is not to be considered by us as obligatory. The ground of moral obligation, as derived from revelation, must, therefore, be a command of God. Now, a command seems to involve three ideas : 1st. That an act be designated ; 2d. That it be somehow signified to be the will of God that this act be performed ; 3d. That it be signified that *we are included* within the number to whom the command is *addressed.* Otherwise, all the commandments to the patriarchs and prophets would be binding upon every one who might read them. And, hence, in general, whosoever urges upon us any duty, as the command of God, revealed in the Bible, must show that God has commanded that action to be done, and that he has commanded us to do it. The mere fact that any thing has been done and recorded in Scripture, by no means places us under obligation to do it. It excludes from being obligatory upon *all*, what has been commanded, but which can be shown to have been intended only for individuals, or for nations, and not for the whole human race. Many of the commands of God in the Old Testament were addressed to *nations.* Such were the directions to the Israelites to take possession of Canaan ; to make war upon the surrounding nations. Of such precepts, it is to be observed : 1st. They are to be obeyed only at the time and in the manner in which they are commanded, and are of force only to those to whom they were given. The New Testament contains all the moral precepts given to man; that is to say, no precept of the Old Testament, which is not either repeated, or its obligations acknowledged, under the new dispensation, is binding upon us at the present day."

Therefore, there is no set of men in America authorized to tell Abraham Lincoln that God required that he should proclaim freedom throughout the land. No man has authority from the Bible to tell him that he sits in the place of Pharaoh, and that God commands him to "Let my people go." These commands have all been made and fulfilled thousands of years before he was born. No man has authority from the Bible to command the people of the North, or teach them that it is their duty to drive out the people of the South, or exterminate them, as Joshua expelled the Canaanites and took possession of their land. Joshua fulfilled God's command at the time it was given; and any other nation or people might, with equal authority, claim the right to expel the Northern people from their soil as they to dispossess the South. Thus, all the teachings of infidels, or of Christians, in this war, contrary to the Bible, are not binding upon the people. Instead of its being Abraham Lincoln's duty to go over to the Old Testament and find out what God said to Pharaoh, or Joshua, or Abraham, or Gideon, Dr. Wayland says "he is bound by moral obligation to obey the Constitution of his country. A government derives its authority from society, of which it is the agent; that society derives its authority from the compact formed by individuals; that society, and the relations between society and individuals, are the ordinance of God. Of course, the officer of a government, as the organ of society, is bound as such by the law of God, and is under obligation to perform the duties of his

office in obedience to this law ; and, hence, it makes no
difference how the other party to the contract executes
their engagements, he, as the servant of God, set apart
for this very thing, is bound, nevertheless, to act precisely according to the principles by which God has declared that this relation should be governed. It is the
duty of a legislator to understand the precise nature of
the compact which binds together the *particular* society
for which he legislates. He who enters upon the duty
of a legislator without a knowledge of the limit of the
several branches of the government, is not only wicked,
but contemptible. He is the worst of all empirics: he
offers to prescribe for a malady, and knows not whether
the medicine he uses be a remedy or a poison. The injury which he inflicts is not on an individual, but on an
entire community. Having acquainted himself with his
powers, and his obligations, he is bound to exert his
power precisely within the limits by which it is restricted,
and for the purpose for which it was conferred, to the
best of his knowledge and ability, and for the best good
of the whole society. He is bound impartially to carry
into effect the principles of the general and the particular
compact just in those *respects* in which the carrying them
into effect is committed to him. For the action of others
he is not responsible, unless he has been made so responsible. He is not the organ of a *section*, or of a *district*, much less of a *party*, but of the *society at large ;*
and he who uses his power for the benefit of a section,
or of a party, is false to his duty, to his country, and his
God. He is engraving his name on the adamantine
pillars of his country's history, to be gazed on forever
as an object of universal detestation.

" It is his duty to leave every thing else undone. From

no plea of necessity, or of peculiar circumstances, may he overstep the limits of his constitutional power, either in the *act itself*, or the *purpose* for which the act is done. The moment he does this, he is a tyrant. Precisely the power *committed* to *him* exists, and *no other*. If he may exercise one power not delegated, he may exercise another, and he may exercise all; thus, on principle, he assumes himself to be the fountain of power; restraint upon encroachment ceases, and all liberty is henceforth at an end."

What an amount of moral guilt, then, rests upon the people who have persuaded Abraham Lincoln to exercise powers not delegated to him by the framers of the Constitution! the original compact upon which the Union and the government was founded, he is the servant of God set apart to execute.

Did Washington, who was one of the framers of that Constitution, delegate authority to Mr. Lincoln to rob the American people of all their slaves, which he called their property, and demanded the restoration, by the British Government, of all such property taken from the citizens of the United States? Can any thing be plainer than this, that the abolitionists, who declared all the laws sanctioning slavery "null and void," have persuaded the President that he can annul the laws at his pleasure. that he is the fountain of all power, and that he derives this power from the present generation, and is not bound to obey the laws made by Washington long years ago? Washington was a father to his people, and the Union would long ere this have been restored, had Mr. Lincoln obeyed his counsels and the Constitution which he made.

It has often been said that General Washington was

a man of prayer. It is unquestionably true. He recognized Jehovah as the God of nations—as the God of battles, and his prayers ascended to heaven for the triumph of the cause of American liberty. There were gloomy periods in the Revolutionary struggle, when the hope of the good man was in God alone. How fervently Washington then prayed! What tears of indignant sorrow he wept over British aggression, and how earnestly he invoked divine interposition in behalf of the oppressed colonies! A soldier in the army, going forth from the camp into a retired spot, saw Washington on his knees in prayer. The sight sent conviction to his heart. He ultimately obtained hope in Christ, and became a devoted Christian. The scene he had witnessed, Washington in prayer, was ever vivid to the eye of his mind. Painters and sculptors have represented Washington in many positions; would it not be well for some of them to picture him on his knees in prayer?

It is assumed by the party now holding the reins of the government which Washington helped to found— the party who declare that they are fighting to preserve the Constitution which Washington helped to frame— that if he were now alive he would be on their side in this bloody contest; that his prayers would ascend to heaven that their policy might succeed, and that he would join with them in declaring that slavery should now be swept away, if every slaveholder, and every man, woman and child should be swept away with it; that this bloody war should never end until the shackles fall from every slave, and universal freedom prevails over America. In 1786, Washington said, "There is not a man living who wishes more sincerely than I do to see a plan adopted for the abolition of slavery; but there is

but one proper and effectual mode by which it can be
accomplished, and that is by legislative authority; and
this, as far as my suffrage will go, shall never be
wanting."

Now here was a warrior who had liberated by his
sword and by his prayers for aid from the God of heaven,
three millions 'of his own race from their yoke of
bondage to the British king; why did he not take this
sword and free the black race in America at the same
time? Why did he not say to Rhode Island, Connecticut, New York, New Jersey, and all the States south
of the Potomac, " I demand immediate and unconditional
emancipation of all your negroes now held in slavery,
or I shall call my soldiers about me and fight for their
liberty?" Was it because he delighted to see them in
bondage? He says, " I hope it will not be conceived
by these observations that it is my wish to hold these
unhappy people in slavery, but there is but one proper
and effectual mode by which it can be accomplished."
No abolitionist at the North had more pity for that
unhappy people than the Father of his Country. They
were always called by the fathers of the republic, " that
unfortunate race ;" but Washington lived fourteen years
after these sentiments were expressed, and yet died
without bestowing liberty upon that people whose
sorrows touched his heart. He lived a quarter of a
century from the day in which he drew his sword in
defence of the white race in America, oppressed by a
tyrannical power exercised over them by the nation from
whence they sprang. He sat eight years in the same
chair of state now occupied by the President engaged in
freeing the slaves left by him in bondage. He had the
same constitutional authority over slavery as that of the

President thus engaged. He felt as much compassion for the negro race thus doomed to the servitude of the white race as Abraham Lincoln now feels, who says, "It seems to me that if any thing is wrong, slavery is wrong." Yet Washington tells Abraham Lincoln, as well as the lawyer to whom he was writing, "There is but one proper and effectual mode by which the abolition of slavery can be accomplished, and that is by legislative authority," by the authority of the legislatures of the several States where slavery is established. They made the laws and they must unmake them with regard to slavery. Now, how came Washington to prescribe this as the only remedy for the evils of slavery? This remedy was given, and this answer written, to counteract the principles and progress of the very party now holding ascendancy over this nation. A society had been formed in Washington's day, as he said, for the very purpose of robbing the Southern people of their slaves, and he declared that that society was acting repugnantly to justice. and that it was only by acts of tyranny and oppression they could accomplish the freedom of the slaves. The abolitionists tell us that "at this time the anti-slavery spirit was very animated, that all classes were imbued with it down even to Tom Paine; yet from that period it became less energetic. Its decline is traced through many years of obscuration, and its revival is attributed to the establishment of the Boston Liberator. in 1831." Why did this anti-slavery spirit become less energetic, and why could its decline be traced through many years of obscuration? Because in their petitions to Congress to free the slaves. these people were told that Congress had no authority given it by the Constitution to interfere with slavery, that each State had sole power over all its own internal concerns. Well, Washington says, " Congress put these abolitionists to sleep, and they would scarcely wake before 1808." He also, it seems, administered an opiate himself which put a stop to their acts of injustice for a time, and they sank into a state of obscuration until 1831. Then the thunders of William Lloyd Garrison revived them from their long slumber. They met together in 1833, and there went forth the cry that the Constitution which would not allow Congress to interfere with slavery was " a covenant with Death and an agreement with hell!" As Washington was out of their way, they gave public notice to the Southern people that they must immediately relinquish all their property in slaves, without any remuneration, or suffer the consequences of a refusal. Washington interfered when they demanded the freedom of one slave without compensation : what would he have said to their demand for the freedom of all on the same condition ? In December, 1862, Abraham Lincoln said:

" The liberation of the slaves is the destruction of property, property acquired by descent or by purchase, the same as any other property. It is no less true for having often been said that the people of the South are no more responsible for the original introduction of their property, than are the people of the North ; and when it is remembered how unhesitatingly we use, all of us, cotton and sugar, and share the profits of dealing in them, it may not be quite safe to say that the South has been more responsible than the North for its continuance. If, then, for a common object, this property is to be sacrificed, is it not just that it be done at a common charge ? And if with less money, or money more easily paid, we can preserve the benefits of the

Union by this means better than by war alone, is it not economical to do it? Is it doubted, then, that the plan I propose would shorten the war, and thus lessen its expenditure of money and blood? Other means may succeed in saving the Union—this could not fail. The way is plain, peaceful, generous, just: a way which, if followed, God must forever bless." The President believed that God would bless the nation in paying for the slaves. But the abolitionists would not accept of such a plan. Four weeks after, Abraham Lincoln was compelled to proclaim freedom to every slave, without compensation or expatriation. These abolitionists assured him that the slaves would all flee from their masters, and the war thus be at an end. They now declare that it shall never end until the proclamation is fulfilled. Would General Washington join the abolitionists in such a war? Would he take sides with men whom he himself rebelled against, as tyrants and oppressors—who have taught the right of his own slaves to run away—to rob and murder him if need be to gain their liberty; and if his wife had stood in the way of their freedom, these negroes, mentioned in his letters, had a natural right to take her life, and that of any member of his family who might stand in their way? If the negroes have a right to murder any master, they had a right to take the life of Washington, or Jefferson, or any other patriot who helped this nation to its independence. If they have a right now to fight for their freedom, they had a right to fight against their masters in Massachusetts, and all the other Eastern States; and as long as one negro remained in slavery, he had a right to kill his master to obtain his freedom. The black race had been in slavery in the colonies more

7

than a hundred years before independence was declared. They had as much right during all that time to rise against the white race as they have at this moment; and if slavery is such a sin in the sight of God, that he has commissioned the North to extirpate it from the land, he might, with equal justice, have authorized some foreign nation to make war on America a hundred years ago, in order to liberate her slaves. That the number is greater now, takes nothing from the argument, for at the time of the Revolution there were more than half a million of slaves, belonging to our forefathers. These had a perfect right, according to the abolitionists, to murder off the white people on this continent; and if their doctrine is true, the present generation ought never to have been born. The negroes should have possessed this country long ago, as they now possess Hayti; and the white people either all exterminated or turned into mulattoes. No! Washington was in favor of the liberty of his own race, and willing to shed his blood to gain their freedom, but never proposed the same to free the negroes, and never advocated the slaughter of the white race for that purpose. It was left for the Republican party to inaugurate such a war; and those who loved and revered Washington turned with horror and disgust at the scenes they are enacting, under the inspiration of Garrison and his followers, whose counsels they follow, and reject the example and warnings of the Father of his Country!

Four years from the time the children of Washington received their last farewell admonitions from his lips, the Senate of the United States addressed the President who succeeded him in the following touching words·

" Permit us, sir, to mingle our tears with yours. On this occasion it is manly to weep. Our country mourns a father. The Almighty Disposer of events has taken from us our greatest benefactor and ornament. With pride we review the life of Washington, and compare him with those of other countries who have been pre-eminent in fame. Ancient and modern names are diminished before him. Greatness and guilt have too often been allied; but his fame is whiter than it is brilliant. The destroyer of nations stood abashed at the majesty of his virtues. Magnanimous in death, the darkness of the grave could not obscure his whiteness. Such was the man we deplore. Thanks to God, his glory is consummated. Washington yet lives on earth in his spotless example—his spirit is in heaven. Let his countrymen consecrate the memory of the heroic general, the patriotic statesman, and the virtuous sage; let them teach their children never to forget that the fruits of his labors and his example are their inheritance."

President Adams replied: " His example is now complete; and it will teach wisdom and virtue to magistrates, citizens, and men, not only in the present age, but in future generations as long as our history shall be read. If Trajan found a Pliny, a Marcus Aurelius can never want biographers, eulogists, or historians." From his home at Mount Vernon, from the capital which bore his name, a wail of sorrow was heard, which was wafted on the breeze all over the sunny South; and soon was borne back to the North, from the shores of South Carolina, the same notes of grief for the loss of a father. In Charleston city, where now is struck down even the youthful maiden, standing before the altar in her bridal robes, by the messenger of death—shot from

cannon, whose boomings still echo, and renew, and pro-
long the wail that told of the death of Washington—a
sermon was preached by the eloquent Richard Furman,
A.M., the first words of which announced that "the
great soul of our beloved Washington has left the world!
Accounts, not to be disputed, have announced his death.
It is an event long to be remembered by Americans.
The melancholy tidings have vibrated on our ears in
saddest accents! They have penetrated our hearts, exciting sensations not to be described; and have produced,
in copious effusion, sincere, but unavailing tears. On
this day, the anniversary of that which gave him to
mankind—the day which, in honor of his virtues, you
were used to devote to festivity and joy—we are met in
the house of God to deplore our loss of him, and to
weep over his urn. On the 14th of December (1799),
and in the sixty-sixth year of his age, he complacently
surrendered his soul into the hands of his Creator.
Washington was to America the valuable gift of God.
Heaven has made him to us both a Moses and a Joshua.
But Washington, the virtuous, the magnanimous, the
brave, the father of his country, is numbered with the
dead!

"Cease to weep, thou virtuous, honored matron, who
hast lost in him the man who ranked with the best of
husbands! Be consoled, ye adopted children, who shared
in him the tenderest father's care! Citizens of America
—his political children—dry your tears! Turn away your
eyes from the desolate mansion, where his presence is no
longer seen. View him in the realms of light, united
in blest society of saints. See him holding high con-
verse with the angels of light, and with them approach-
ing the Divine Presence in humble adoration, perfecting

in high, immortal strains, those grateful acknowledgments of the Divine interposition, goodness, and mercy, which he began here on earth, while youth smiles in his face, joy beams in his eye, and his brows are bound, not with a wreath of fading laurel, but with the branches of the tree of life and flowers of paradise!"

And why is that same city, where the people then met to weep over the urn of Washington, again blockaded as in the dark days when he was fighting to free its captive citizens from the power of their British foes? Why are the people of the whole South now in rebellion against Abraham Lincoln and the abolition party, as they were then in rebellion against George the Third and his tyrannical ministers? Why are the beautiful plains of the South overspread with blood and carnage; and why has the home of Mary, the mother of Washington, been thrice drenched in human gore? Why are the white brothers of the great family of the Father of his Country still engaged in a war of direst hate, and seeking to plunge the dagger into each other's heart, instead of loving one another, and living together in peace, in the Union which he perilled his life to establish for their inheritance forever? Because, that, in just sixty years from the moon in which his spirit entered the portals of bliss, the abolition brothers tore the laurels from his brow and placed them on the head of "Old John Brown!" Because they robbed him of his titles to the name and offices of a Moses and a Joshua, and gave them to the chieftain of a robber band! Because they disowned and repudiated their own father, and set up in his place a false prophet, who proclaimed that he had a mission from God Almighty to put their white brothers South to death, and give their lands to their negro slaves, and that between the command of the Lord of Hosts and implicit obedience to it, he permitted no constitution nor law to intervene. The Union and the Constitution which Washington founded were the two lions in his way; but he marched straight ahead, trampling under foot the rotten stubble of unjust laws and constitutions that stood between him and his foes. This was the prophet the abolitionists had been long looking for, and praying for his appearing. When he came, they said that, " during the eighteen centuries which have passed, no such character has appeared among men ; that the galleries of the resounding ages echo with no footfall mightier than that of the martyr who stepped from the scaffold into the embrace of angels." They teach the children of the nation to sing his praises, instead of obeying the injunction of the Senate, to teach them never to forget that their own liberties were the fruits of the labor and toil of the Father of his Country. They have learned the soldiers, who are fighting for the Union, to hymn their peans to John Brown, while the Moses who led their fathers through the Revolution and planted them in the land of freedom is unhonored and unsung. They point the nation up to heaven, not there to behold the Father of his Country enwreathed with flowers of Paradise, but to view the criminal executed for breaking laws of his own enacting, among the spirits of the blest, mustering a cohort of these invisible beings into his abolition army, and leading them against the people of the South, whom he failed to exterminate while here in the flesh.

But why do the abolitionists reverence the name of John Brown above that of Washington? What glorious deeds place his name so much higher on the roll of fame

than that of the warrior who gave freedom to America?
If history has recorded his noble achievements, let them
be compared with those of the Father of his Country,
whose laurels they have trampled in the dust. Here
is a record of October, 1859, by Horace Greeley, now
fighting under his banners:

" Old Brown, of Ossawatamie, who was last heard of
on his way to Canada with a band of runaway slaves
from Missouri, now turns up in Virginia, where he has
been some months plotting and preparing for a general
stampede of slaves. The insurrection at Harper's Ferry
proves a verity."

This was the Moses of the abolitionists. "No such
character had appeared for eighteen hundred years
among mankind." The fame of Rob Roy sinks in in-
significance by the side of the daring exploits of the
band of midnight robbers of old John Brown. His
armed banditti captured the sword and the pistols of
General Washington himself, presented to him by
Frederick the Great and the Marquis de Lafayette, and
more than this, they captured the heir to his name and
to his earthly estates. No wonder he can gather a
cohort of infernal spirits to assist in this war of subjugation and extermination! Let the captive prisoner in
whose veins flowed the blood of Washington, relate to
us this brilliant victory, which throws all the battles of
the Father of his Country against the King of Great
Britain into the shades.

" I was awakened in the night by hearing my name
called. I opened the door, and before me stood four
men, three of them armed with Sharpe's rifles, levelled
and cocked, and the other with a revolver in his right
hand, and a lighted flambeau in the other. They said

to me, ' Is your name Washington ?' I answered, ' That is my name.'   I was then told that I was a prisoner, and not to be frightened.   I replied, ' Do you see any thing that looks like fright about me ?'   They said, ' If you surrender, and come with us freely, you are safe.'   I was told to put on my clothes, and I said, ' While I am dressing, you will please tell me what all this means.' One said, ' We want your arms,' and I opened the gun-closet for them to help themselves.   They then explained their mission, to wit: The emancipation of all the slaves in the country.   Stephens said: ' Have you got any money ?'   I replied: ' I wish I had a great deal.'   ' Be careful, sir,' said he.   ' Have you a watch ?'   My reply was, ' I have, but you cannot have it.   You have set yourselves up as great moralists and liberators of slaves. Now it appears that you are robbers as well.' "

General Washington pronounced the abolitionists in his day tyrants and oppressors.   His grand-nephew, Colonel John A. Washington, pronounced them robbers as well, and had he known their history at that moment he might have added, " and murderers likewise."

" I told them I was dressed and ready to go.   They bade me wait a short time and my carriage would be at the door.   They had ordered my carriage for me, and pried open the stable door to get it out.   My servant drove my horses.   I suspected they were only robbers, and would turn off at some point, but they drove directly to the United States Armory at Harper's Ferry.   They said they intended freely to appropriate the property of slaveholders to carry out their plans of freeing the negroes.

" They seized all of Colonel Washington's slaves within their reach, and those on the other plantations near,

and made their owners prisoners also. They expected
to be speedily reinforced, first, by the slaves in Canada,
and, secondly, by the slaves in the South. They were
to be armed with pikes, scythes, shot-guns, and other
simple instruments of defence. The officers, white and
black, and such of the negroes as were skilled, to have
the use of Sharpe's rifles and revolvers. They antici-
pated procuring provisions enough for subsistence by
forage, as also arms and horses and ammunition, and thus
sweep every plantation in the South."* Turn now to
the horrors of St. Domingo, and view a faint picture of
the scenes which this Moses of the abolitionists was preparing to re-enact among the white people of the South.
And for this glorious undertaking they declare that " he
stepped from the gallows into the embrace of angels."
After the danger was over, the South asks, " Did he not
train his sons to aid him in his attempt to waste with
fire and sword the fairest land under the cope of heaven ?
How many sisters did he propose to murder ? How
many social hearths to quench in blood ? For what
use were these hundreds of deadly rifles, those loads of
pikes, those bundles of incendiary faggots ? A felon's
death ! Almighty Providence ! Is man indeed so weak
that he can inflict no more ?"

And what punishment is due to the abolitionists of
the North who would see their white brothers and
sisters of the South exterminated, and their lands given
over to their negroes ? Yet for these awful attempts
and designs of John Brown, they offer up their hymns
of adoration and praise, and let it be remembered that
the Southern people were not then rebels, and that name

---

* Redpath's Life of John Brown and his Trial.

could not be used in justification of the murderous designs of the abolitionists; but they were slaveholders, and these abolitionists declared that God commanded that slaveholders should be put to death. Redpath says, " If the Bible is God's true word, it follows that it is right to slay God's enemies." The Southern people were held up to the world as the enemies of God, and that it was a Christian duty to exterminate them, before one single man among them rebelled against the government. It is against these "tyrants," these "oppressors," these "robbers and murderers" that they are to-day in arms. Every method has been tried by these fiends in human shape to produce a massacre in the South precisely like that in St. Domingo, and they are to-day lamenting over the failure of a plan said to be defeated by Generals Rosecrans and Garfield. They say, "It was a gigantic project; the trains were all laid, the matches all lighted, and two centuries of cruel wrong were about to be avenged in a night, when a white man said to the negro, ' You will slaughter friends and enemies. You will wade deep in innocent blood. God cannot be with you in midnight massacre.' A white man said that, and the uplifted torch fell from the negro's hand, and while the Southern men were starving our prisoners, butchering our wounded and desecrating our dead, we were supplicating the destroying angel to pass over their homes, and save their wives and little ones from swift destruction. In the day when ' He maketh inquisition for blood,' on whose garments, my Southern brothers, think you will he find the stain?"

That question, " my *abolition brothers*," is already answered. You would have rejoiced to see those " wives and little ones involved in swift destruction," not because they have rebelled against the government; for you declared the United States Government so wicked that none should obey it; but because you have hated your white brothers, and loved the negroes; and following the example of your brother infidels in France—Marat and Cloots—you formed the mad and wicked project of spreading your doctrines of equality among the white and black races, between whom, says Washington, through his beloved friend, there exist distinctions and prejudices to be subdued only by the grave. And you can coolly and deliberately pursue your baneful theories through oceans of blood; you could see a preconcerted insurrection of the blacks throughout the whole South; you could see the white inhabitants, while sleeping peacefully in their beds, involved in one indiscriminate slaughter, from which neither age nor sex could afford an exemption. And General Washington, were he now alive, would furnish arms and ammunition to quell the insurrection, which you would rejoice to see successful; and punish the men who taught these wicked doctrines —and the Almighty knows on whose garments is the blood of this nation. John Brown was struck dead on the very threshold of his enterprise. The Almighty has proven by this that the Moses of the abolitionists was a lying prophet—that the commission he pretended to have received from the Lord was a forgery; and yet the abolitionists delivered these spurious commands, this forged commission of the false prophet, into the hands of Abraham Lincoln, and declared to him that the Almighty placed him in power, and gave him the sword of John Brown, for the express purpose of setting free the whole four millions of negro slaves. For three years " the soul of John Brown has been marching on," until the "fairest land under the cope of heaven has been wasted with fire and sword, and thousands of social hearths, both North and South, have been quenched in blood;" and still the war goes on. .

Let the people invoke the spirit of Washington to come to their aid and subdue the spirit of Old John Brown! Washington still lives in heaven, his brows still bound with branches of the tree of life "which is given for the healing of the nations." He is an angel of light: John Brown an angel of darkness; Washington is an angel of mercy and peace: John Brown is an angel of vengeance and destruction; Washington was the incarnation of goodness: John Brown the incarnation of evil; Washington was the good angel that presided over the Union and the Constitution: John Brown was the demon that rose out of the bottomless pit, bearing in his hands the banner inscribed with the motto, written in blood, "The Constitution of the United States is a Covenant with Death and an Agreement with Hell." Washington said, "I never expect to draw my sword again. I can scarcely conceive the cause that would induce me to do it. My first wish is to see the whole world in peace, and its inhabitants as one band of brothers. As mankind become more enlightened and humanized, I cannot but flatter myself with the pleasing prospect that more pacific systems will take place among men."

But the disciples of John Brown will have no peace; they will not have the white people of the South for their brothers; they are not yet enlightened, nor yet humanized, and they say, "We will have no pacification, no conciliation, no negotiation, but only subjugation, and this war shall never end until every slave is free, although a million garments more are rolled in blood."

Abraham Lincoln is the representative of John Brown. Let the people take the sceptre from his hand and place it in the hands of a representative of Washington. Let them bring fresh laurels and crown the Father of his Country anew. The abolitionists have trodden his glories in the dust! They have delivered into the hands of John Brown the trophies of his greatness. They have veiled his statue in a drapery of mourning. They have driven his children into exile, and scoff at the principles which they derived from their father. Let the people of the North, who love him, rally to his standard. Let them recount his glorious deeds on the field of battle, and renew the stories of his sufferings and toils in achieving the liberty of his country. Let them bear aloft a banner that will reach even unto the skies, and holding it before the burning throne, may his image be so impressed upon the silken folds that its brightness may be reflected over the whole land he once delighted to call his own. Let his children in the South behold the face of their father, with his kind, benignant smile, beckoning them to return to the Union. And let them see that they have brothers and sisters in the North who love them better than their negro slaves, and would welcome their return! Then will the rebellious children no longer rebel. They will lay down their arms, and come with tears of penitence and joy to the embrace of their brothers, who still acknowledge the same father, and renew their allegiance to the government of the great, the brave, the magnanimous, the immortal George Washington, the Father of the American Republic.

"Oh, yes! thy counsels shall be heard, oh Washington! Oh warrior! Oh legislator! Oh citizen without reproach! The acclamations of every age will be offered to the hero who gave freedom and happiness to his country! The people who so lately stigmatized Washington as a rebel, regard even the enfranchisement of America as one of those events consecrated by history, and by past ages. Such is the veneration excited by great characters. The mourning which Napoleon orders for Washington, declares to France that Washington's example is not lost. It is less for the illustrious general, than for the benefactor of a great people, that the crape of mourning now covers our banners, and the uniform of our warriors. Amid all the excesses of a civil war, humanity took refuge in his tent, and was never repulsed. In triumph, or defeat, he was tranquil as wisdom, as pure as virtue. The finer feelings of his heart never abandoned him, even in those moments when his own interests would seem to justify a recourse to the laws of vengeance."—*Funeral Oration on Washington, delivered in the Temple of Mars, Paris. By Lewis Fontanes.*

But among all the brave chieftains of the North, oh Washington, who is like unto thee? Unto whom, oh Father of our nation, has been transmitted the virtues which made thine own name illustrious and immortal? In whose soul now shines the same moral beauties which painters and sculptors declared were reflected from thine own countenance, the civic and humane holding ascendency over thy military virtues, making thy features radiant with benevolence and moral loveliness? Unto whom has there descended the genius, the bravery, and the undaunted courage which triumphed at last over a кingdom and a throne? And oh ye children of America! is there now among you a living representative of the character and principles of the Father of your Country, he who gathered you together in one fold, secure from the paw of the *Lion*, and bade you live in love and peace in the Union he established for you forever?

Yes, his name is on the air! The people have descried him! The true political son of Washington! His own similitude! George B. McClellan! The resemblance so plain, so distinct, that the followers of John Brown, recognizing it, tore the laurels, which he had won in fighting for the Union, immediately from his brow, as they had torn those of Washington three years before, deprived him of his command, exiled him from the soldiers of his army whom he loved, trampled his honors in the dust, enveloped his name in a cloud of falsehood and detraction, and consigned him, as they fondly hoped, to the dark shades of oblivion. Two years pass away, and they start up with affected surprise and ask the question, "Who is General McClellan, that has been nominated for President of the United States! Oh, he is that military adventurer who came to Washington, and whom President Lincoln drew from obscurity, and placed in command of the army. It was another officer than he that planned and executed the brilliant achievements which at first were credited to him." Thus, the tyrants and oppressors who robbed the Southern people of their property in Washington's own day, who robbed his namesake at midnight of his watch, his silver, his carriage and horses, of the sword presented by Frederick the Great, and the pistols presented by General Lafayette, have not scrupled to rob General McClellan of his titles to honor, and of his credentials establishing his claims to the office of President of the United States. The very fact of their endeavors to conceal them prove that if they can be found his claims will be undisputed, and it then remains for the people to choose for their President a representative of Washington, or of old John Brown.

The very name of Washington was hailed with joy and blessings; benedictions and praises fell thick upon his head. And so with the name of McClellan. On the 15th day of July, 1861, these words were recorded in the city of Washington:

"Your name, General McClellan, was on lips yesterday counted by millions. God bless you! Your battles are not to be estimated by any count of killed or prisoners. The whole people start up from doubt and despondency, and hail the breaking day for which they have waited with slow and counted hours. Yesterday was a happy day in Washington, even to hilarity. (It was Sunday). We sent up aspirations of thanksgiving for the victories in Western Virginia."

"Congress hastens to send forth from the Capitol a greeting of 'thanks to General George B. McClellan and the officers and soldiers under his command, for the series of brilliant and decisive victories which they, by their skill and bravery, achieved over the rebels and traitors in the army on the battle-fields of Western Virginia.'"

General Washington's army was proud of their leader, and so was General McClellan's. The officers in Western Virginia said, "We feel very proud of our wise and brave young major-general. There is a future before him, if his life is spared, which he will make illustrious."

Virginia was proud to be called the birth-place of

Washington, and Philadelphia was proud to claim the
city as the birth-place of General McClellan.   The
Press says:

"The brilliant victories which have recently been
achieved by General McClellan have justly rendered
him one of the most popular officers in our army, and
justified all the high expectations which had been
entertained by those who knew his sterling qualities.
Before his advancing forces and their resistless attacks,
the insurgents fly in terror; but even then, his combina-
tions are of such a character that they do not escape, for
he has already taken more than a thousand prisoners,
and, with but a small loss among his own forces, killed
two hundred and fifty of the enemy, including General
Garnett, one of their most distinguished officers.

"These results are peculiarly gratifying to our citizens,
not only on account of the important influence they will
have in deciding the struggle in which the patriots of
the nation are engaged, but because we are proud to
claim General McClellan as a Philadelphian, and because
it is well understood that they are due, not to accident,
but in a great measure to his military genius.   No young
man in our country has taken greater pains to render
himself a thorough soldier.   He not only attained high
distinction in different branches of service before the
war commenced, but by close personal inspection of all
the Russian, French, and English camps, during the
Crimean war, thoroughly familiarized himself with all
the important phases of modern warfare.

"Devotedly attached to the Union, all the energies of
his nature have been enlisted in the present struggle to
preserve it; and he has displayed in all his movements
since it commenced, a degree of zeal, energy, courage and

8

sagacity, deserving of great credit. The completeness of his preparations, doubtless, aided materially to insure his success; and he evinced, in organizing his forces, the same skill, which, when he fairly encountered the enemy, produced such glorious triumphs. The officers of the rebel army have been heard to express serious apprehensions of the fate that awaited them, after General McClellan's column fairly commenced operations in Western Virginia. If his life is spared, his name will doubtless continue to strike terror into every traitor's breast, as long as an armed foe to our government treads our soil."

And that is the man they now call a traitor, a sympathizer with the rebels, because he was determined to preserve the Constitution and Union, as the Father of his Country commanded him to do.

As Washington was sent for in haste to come to the relief of Boston, so General McClellan was summoned in haste to protect Washington.

On July 22d, 1861, Horace Greeley said: " We have fought and been beaten. (God forgive our rulers that it is so.) The sacred soil of Virginia is crimson and wet with the blood of thousands of Northern men, needlessly shed. An indignant people will demand the immediate retirement of the present cabinet. Give the President capable advisers, and leaders for the army worthy the rank and file. The people will insist upon having the best generals, captains, and colonels the country can furnish."

24th. " General McClellan has been summoned from Western Virginia to take command of the Army of the Potomac."

" Philadelphia, July 25.—General Geo. B. McClellan,

Commandant of the Grand Army of the Potomac, left Beverly on Tuesday, and rode forty miles on horseback to Grafton, where he took the cars for Wheeling. On his arrival at Pittsburg, he was received with the greatest *eclat* by the people. The military, firemen, and citizens, turned out to meet him, and several salutes were fired in his honor. Upon arriving in this city, the cars which are pulled by horses from the Schuylkill into town were surrounded by a wild mob, cheering, yelling, and climbing the platforms. A carriage, guarded by policemen, was waiting at the depot. A regiment of Reserve Grays escorted the barouche, and General McClellan was obliged to stand over the whole route, and bow, hat-in-hand, to the thousands of faces and salutations. Bouquets were showered upon him from the ladies at the windows, and all the bunting on Chestnut and Spruce streets was displayed. His carriage was loaded down with flowers. General McClellan passed his boyhood in Philadelphia, and the people were disposed to lay the whole merit of his career to that fact."

Yes, General McClellan is brave, valiant, heroic, like unto Washington, and the same honors strew his path; but who shall unfold to public view the virtues of his heart? All are proud to do him homage—all eager to speak forth his praises—is there one who can portray the beauties of his mind and heart? Yes, to a listening throng, gathered in the capital of the nation, General Ambrose Burnside pronounced this eulogy upon his friend. Said the speaker:

"I have known General McClellan intimately; we were students together, soldiers together in the field, private citizens together for years. No feeling of ambition beyond the good of his country, and the success

of her cause, ever entered his breast. We have lived
together in the same family. I know him as well as I
know any human being on the face of the earth. No
more honest, conscientious man exists than General
McClellan. (Applause.) All that he does is with a
single view for the success of this government and the
breaking down of this rebellion. Nothing under the
sun would ever induce him to swerve from what he
knows to be his duty. He is an honest, conscientious,
Christian-like man. And I would add, he has the
soundest head, and the clearest military perception of
any man in the United States. (A cry—'Western Virginia.') A more brilliant short campaign was never
enacted than that of Western Virginia. He need not
be ashamed of his work there, and the country need
never be ashamed of any work he might ever have to
do." (Applause.) Yes, he has the virtues as well as the
genius of Washington.

August 1st, 1861, Horace Greeley wrote: "Ten days
ago the confusion and apparent demoralization of the
troops at Washington, after the disaster at Bull Run,
caused a pall of gloom to settle over the capital city,
and here, and elsewhere. The dull, leaden feeling which
follows a bitter reverse oppressed all men, and very few
thought of the future with springing hope. Now, in
this day all is changed, and the chief cause of this
changed atmosphere is the confidence felt in Washington by the advent of the young general who is called to
command the army, and the admirable system of dis-
cipline he has put in force."

Special Dispatch.—"It is said by those who profess
to know, that the credit of calling General McClellan to

the command of the Army of the Potomac belongs to President Lincoln."

And this is the "military adventurer whom Mr. Lincoln drew from his obscurity!"   "Oh, shame! where is thy blush?"

General Washington demanded of the British that the Revolutionary War should be conducted upon the highest principles of civilization, and complained that "the appellation of rebels to the Americans was deemed sufficient to sanctify every species of cruelty to them." In reply to a letter from him on this subject, Sir Guy Carleton wrote as follows:

"Sir:—It is with me to declare, that if war must prevail, I shall endeavor to render its miseries as light to the people of this continent as the circumstances of such a condition will possibly permit.   How much soever we may differ in other respects, upon this one point we must perfectly concur; being alike interested to preserve the name of Englishman from reproach, and individuals from experiencing such unnecessary evils as can have no effect upon a general decision."

Washington demanded that every soldier who should be caught pillaging, plundering, or burning a dwelling, should be punished; and said that death itself was not too great a punishment in such a case.   But the abolitionists demanded the removal of General McClellan for not wishing to bring reproach upon the descendants of the family of Washington, and disgracing the name of American.   If General McClellan was a rose-water general, so was Washington.   The name of rebel has sanctified outrages for which the Almighty will hold the North, as well as the South, to strict account.

General Washington had his enemies and persecutors,

and so has General McClellan. A writer says: " When a man is compelled to contend with enemies from without, and with enemies from within—with those even of his own household as well as with the foe in the field— he certainly deserves the sympathies of every liberal and magnanimous mind."

" This is the fate of the young and distinguished officer, who, on the retirement of General Scott, was called upon to succeed him, with all the great and fearful responsibilities of the chief command. But the fortune of General McClellan is not a singular one. The great Burke has truly said that ' censure is the tax a man pays to the public for being eminent.' Even the noble and unequalled Washington, in the darkest days of the Revolution, was assailed by malignant envy, and a conspiracy formed to remove him. His great soul was troubled, not only for his country, but his countrymen; and the descendants of those who abused and conspired against Washington are now abusing and conspiring against McClellan. We are not instituting any comparisons between men, but draw on history for illustrations. We have judged General McClellan, not as a Democrat, or a Republican. We have but recently learned that he is called a Democrat. We have judged him only as a general and a soldier. When he achieved those brilliant victories in Western Virginia, his name rung through the land. Why should he be condemned because he is at the head of the Army of the Potomac? Nothing that he does, or does not do, satisfies his enemies. We have no prejudices for or against General McClellan, but we are disgusted, nay, indignant at the bitter, unrelenting personal attacks upon him, conflicting in their charges, and only agreeing in their rancor and hate. Attacks which tend to give aid and comfort to the enemy. We look upon these assaults of General McClellan, and, through him, on the government, as treason, moral, if not political and legal, against the country."—*Binghamton Republican*, 1862.

Washington prayed for his country, and so does General McClellan. "Dr. Thompson of the Second Presbyterian Church, Cincinnati, relates that he was recently seated in his study, when a gentleman requested an interview, which was granted. He came to talk about his country, expressing his anxiety about its condition, and at length requested the Doctor to pray for the Republic and for him. The Doctor complied. And after further conversation on this theme, the gentleman requested the minister to pray *with* him. They knelt upon the floor, and the visitor, in a devout and eloquent petition, invoked the aid and protection of the Almighty in this great struggle in which the Republic is involved. 'My visitor,' said Dr. Thompson, 'was Major-General George B. McClellan. It was the most touching and unaffected incident I ever witnessed.'" — *Religious Herald*, 1861.

LETTER FROM GENERAL McCLELLAN TO BISHOP WHIPPLE:

HEADQUARTERS ARMY OF THE POTOMAC,
September, 1862.

MY DEAR BISHOP—Will you do me the favor to perform Divine Service in my camp this evening? If you can give me a couple of hours notice, I shall be glad, that I may be able to inform the corps in the vicinity. After the great success that God has vouchsafed us, I feel that we cannot do less than avail ourselves of the first opportunity to render to him the thanks that are due to him alone. I, for one, feel that the great result is the result of his great mercy ; and would be glad that you should be the medium to offer the thanks I feel due to him from this army, and from the country.

Earnestly hoping you will accede to my request,

I am, very respectfully, your humble servant,

GEO. B. McCLELLAN, *Maj. Gen. Commanding.*

FREDERICK, MD., *September* 27, 1862.

MY DEAR GENERAL—I have spent the day in visiting your brave boys who are in the hospital here. I had the privilege to visit the wayside hospitals between here and the camps. I am sure it will gladden your heart—and it surely did my own—to see the great love they have to you. When I told them how tenderly you had spoken of them, and how you knelt with me in prayer for God's blessing upon them, many a brave fellow wept for joy; and on every side I heard, "God bless the General ;" while here and there some veteran claimed the privilege to say, "God bless little Mac." I had the opportunity to commend some dying men to God, and to whisper the Saviour's name in their ear for their last journey.

If I did not fear of wearying you, I could write an hour, telling you of words of loving confidence spoken by these brave sufferers, who have been with you in good and evil report. I will not. But I cannot close without telling you how sweet is the remembrance of the pleasant service held in your camp, nor to assure you that it is a pleasure every day to ask God to bless you. Your way is rough. Many do not know you. Many are jealous of your success. Many will try to fetter you. But let no cloud above, or thorn beneath, trouble you. Above you is God our Father, Christ our Saviour, the Holy Ghost our Comforter. God will hear our prayers. It may be a weary, foot-sore way, but there is light beyond. God bless you.

I am, with love, your servant, for Christ's sake,

H. B. WHIPPLE.

www.ingramcontent.com/pod-product-compliance
Lightning Source LLC
Chambersburg PA
CBHW020759020726
47495CB00008B/2500